THE WEDDING
DARE

46

Get **more** out of libraries

Please return or renew this item by the last date shown.
You can renew online at www.hants.gov.uk/library
Or by phoning 0845 603 5631

HANNAY

Hampshire
County Council

THE WEDDING DARE

BY

BARBARA HANNAY

MILLS & BOON®

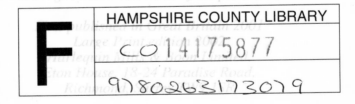

Published in Great Britain 2001
Large Print edition 2002
Harlequin Mills & Boon Limited,
Eton House, 18-24 Paradise Road,
Richmond, Surrey TW9 1SR

ISBN 0 263 17307 0

Set in Times Roman 16½ on 18 pt.
16-0602-44637

Printed and bound in Great Britain
by Antony Rowe Ltd, Chippenham, Wiltshire

CHAPTER ONE

THERE was really only one man in the mall who would look good taking his clothes off. Laura Goodman could tell at a glance that the fellow lounging against the letter box just outside the coffee shop was the man she'd been sent to collect.

He had all the important credentials—broad shoulders and indecently developed biceps straining the stretch cotton of his T-shirt, lean hips and long legs encased in denim.

Even from this distance she could see that his skin was tanned and glowing and, although she couldn't see his face, his bearing suggested supreme confidence.

From her parked car, Laura scanned the rest of the mall entrance. Every other male in the vicinity was pimply or pudgy, balding or under age. This guy had to be the male stripper.

She turned off the ignition and took a steadying breath as she pushed her car door open. It was all very well for Susie and the girls to delegate her to chauffeur this fellow because they knew she could be relied on to stay sober for the whole evening. But there was more than one reason why she shouldn't be sauntering into the mall to pick up a strange man.

If tonight's party hadn't been a hen-night for her best friend, and if she wasn't Susie's bridesmaid, Laura would not have ventured out mid-week at all.

Right now, she should be on the end of a telephone, trying every agent in Brisbane to find a replacement clown for tomorrow's book-reading session at the children's hospital. That was a task more in keeping with her recent promotion to senior librarian and a much more worthy cause than providing Susie and her friends with coarse entertainment.

Laura sighed as she straightened her uncomfortable dress and set off across the mall's uneven paving stones. Keeping her spiky high heels out of the cracks required most of her concentration, but one corner of her mind also tussled with the problem of tomorrow at the children's ward.

Just before she'd left home this evening, she'd had a phone call from her regular assistant to tell her he'd come down with a virus and wouldn't be able to do the clown stint.

Last week she'd promised the children she'd bring them a clown to accompany her weekly book-reading and they'd been ecstatic. Now it would be almost impossible to find a replacement in time.

She might have delayed leaving for the party while she made some calls, but Susie had cornered her at work earlier in the afternoon asking if she would "be a darling" and make a detour via the mall on her way to make an important pick-up.

A pair of faded blue jeans entered Laura's line of vision and she came to an abrupt halt. She'd reached her target.

The stripper.

He was mere inches away, still slouching against the letter box.

Time to forget about children's wards and clowns.

Never having met a stripper before—male or female—Laura pressed her lips together before smiling gingerly. "Good evening." She always made a habit of being polite, no matter whom she addressed.

"Evening."

The rich timbre of his voice startled her. In fact, its resonance was so surprising that, just for a moment, Laura couldn't think of what to say next. Especially when the man levered his noteworthy body away from the letter box and stood tall and erect, looking down at her with a distinctly guarded expression.

He crossed his arms over his chest and frowned at her.

Laura hesitated.

Up close, his face was much nicer looking than she'd expected. Maybe she'd stereotyped strippers, but she hadn't figured on finding such obvious intelligence in those wary grey eyes. His dark hair was thick and shiny and, although he hadn't bothered to shave, she could see the line of a very strong, resolute jaw through his dark stubble.

She struggled with the problem of how best to address him. It wasn't appropriate to blurt out, ''Are you the stripper?''

And yet she had to say something.

Clearly she was taking too long. He was scowling at her as if she was something sloppy a bird had dropped.

''You looking for someone?'' he asked suddenly.

''Er—yes!'' Laura tried to cover her surprise by giving a little shrug of her shoulder.

She swung her evening bag casually from its silk string handles, hoping to look as sophisticated and cool as any of her friends who were, right at this moment, recklessly tossing down far too many champagne cocktails at Susie's party and leaving her to do their dirty work.

Laura smiled bravely. ''Yes, I'm expecting to meet someone here. Actually—'' she arched an eyebrow and sent him another courageous smile ''—I'm pretty certain I'm here to meet you.''

His eyes gleamed. ''Well, I'm sorry to disappoint you, sweetheart, but my entertainment's already planned for this evening—and it's usually free.''

For a long moment Laura stared at him as the full meaning of his reply sank in. Did he think she was—?

''Oh, no!'' she cried. ''You can't possibly imagine—'' She jumped back quickly, one of her heels hit a crack in the paving and her ankle caved in beneath her.

Her arms flailed in the air and the clasp of her handbag caught him square on the chin.

He grunted a muffled curse.

Laura's heels made a noisy clatter on the paving stones as she struggled to regain her balance and to keep her handbag under control. Finally she was upright and steady.

As he rubbed his dark chin the man's frown deepened. He looked as if he couldn't believe what had just happened.

She reached out a tentative hand, but left it hovering in mid-air. ''I'm so sorry.''

''I'll live,'' he muttered, and shoved his hands deep into the pockets of his jeans. He looked around him, as if he hoped there was someone nearby who would lay claim to this annoying woman.

"I was trying to say that I'm not—what you were thinking," Laura hastened to explain. "I'm here to pick you up. Not pick you up *that* way. I'm here to take you to the party."

"Party?"

"Yes. Susie asked me to give you a lift. The mall is on my way."

"You mean Susie Thomson, Rob Parker's fiancée?" For the first time, the shadowy doubt in his grey eyes lightened a little.

"Yes."

"*She* arranged my lift? I was planning to take a taxi because we'll be drinking, but Rob insisted someone would pick me up."

Laura shrugged. "I was the lucky person commissioned to fetch you." To her relief, after he'd considered this news for a lengthy moment, he seemed to relax at last.

In fact, he shrugged his mighty shoulders and actually smiled. "Let's not waste any time, then. Take me to the party."

*　　*　　*

She looked like a feather duster on legs, Nick decided, as he followed his escort back across the mall. Of course, he had to admit they were extremely classy legs. Almost as classy as her dark auburn hair and deep blue eyes.

But that was more than he could say for her astonishing dress. It seemed to be nothing more than a long boa of blue feathers that she'd wound around her.

With her sensuous body and her vampish taste in clothes, it was no wonder he'd thought she was a hooker. Most men would take one look at that reel of feathers and think about unwinding them.

One or two feathers drifted away from her now as she deactivated the central locking system on her smart little sedan.

''Hop in and you'll be at the party in a jiffy,'' she said.

Nick lowered his long body into the passenger seat.

She turned the key in the ignition. ''You can adjust that to give you more leg-room.''

''Thanks.'' At a touch, the seat slid back. ''Nice car.''

"It's new and I'm very proud of it. I bought it to celebrate my promotion."

Her pride showed in the way she smoothly manoeuvred the vehicle out into the traffic flow. Nick enjoyed driving and he admired this woman's skill. She'd had a promotion. Maybe she wasn't a sandwich short of a picnic after all.

As she neatly switched lanes, she shot him a shy smile. "I should call you something. What er—what name do you use—at parties?"

"I beg your pardon?"

"I imagine you might like to keep your working life separate for—er—personal—for privacy. Maybe you have a pseudonym?"

"For *parties?*"

"Yes."

Nick gaped at her. "Do *you* have a special name just for parties?"

"Oh, no!" she cried. "But I told you, I'm not—" She cut off her response as she stamped down on the brake. They'd reached a traffic light.

In the glare of the overhead lights, Nick could see that this girl looked as mixed-up as she sounded. He revised his assessment of her. This was one confused cookie.

"Look," he sighed as they headed off again, "the name's Nick...at parties...at work...at home. I'm afraid I'm Nick Farrell twenty-four hours a day, seven days a week."

She cracked a brief smile. "Hi, Nick. I'm Laura. Laura Goodman."

"Laura," he repeated, and he realised that when he'd met her in the Glenwood mall he'd expected a more exotic name. Now, sitting beside her, inhaling a delicate hint of rose and jasmine and observing the prim, uncomfortable expression on her face, almost as if she were afraid of him, an old-world name like Laura Goodman made more sense.

She swung her car into a kerbside space, behind a string of other parked vehicles. "Here we are."

Nick frowned. "This isn't Rob's street."

"Rob?" Laura frowned back. "But we're going to Susie's. Rob's the groom."

He stared at her. "Rob's having his bucks' party at Susie's?"

"No, of course not. Susie's having her hen-party here. Actually, she's calling it *frock-tails.*" She rolled her eyes and gestured down at her feathers. "That's why I'm dressed like this. Susie wanted all her girlfriends drinking cocktails in frocks. Get it? *Frock*tails? The crazier the frock, the better. Of course I don't actually drink—"

Nick interrupted her. "I *don't* get it. What I particularly don't get is why you've brought *me* here!"

Laura's blue eyes widened. "But you're the—the VIP guest."

A VIP guest at a hen-night? Sweat broke out all over him.

Clearly Laura Goodman *had* lost her marbles. He quickly considered his options. He could scramble out of her car, run for the nearest phone box and call a cab, or he could put his nose in the door at this *frocktail* party and confront Susie, his best mate's fiancée. He didn't know her all that well, but she seemed pretty level-headed.

Surely she could sort out this mess.

Laura leaned closer and her expression showed distaste warring with sympathetic, motherly concern. "Come inside," she urged gently. "Susie organised this. She'll explain. All I know is I had to bring you here."

"She'd damn well better sort this out," he growled as he pushed the passenger door open.

On the footpath, he took deep breaths of summer night air. The sounds of hysterical girlish laughter and popular music pulsated from a brightly lit house nearby.

Closer at hand, he heard a different sound. "Oh, *no!*"

Still standing on the other side of her car, Laura was clutching at her chest while one hand waggled in the air behind her as she tried to reach an elusive trail of feathers. Nick could see that her feathers had snagged as she climbed out of the car and her incredible excuse for a dress was coming undone. He had a clear view of a wispy lace undergarment and her super-soft, pale back shimmering in the moonlight.

"Oh, for pity's sake!" she wailed, sounding and looking panic stricken.

Nick stepped around the back of the vehicle. "Allow me."

Not giving her time to object, he picked up the offending string of feathers and drew them firmly in place across her back.

"It's OK," she cried. "Please—you don't have to bother. I can manage."

He ignored her fretful flapping. "What happens now?" he asked gruffly, walking around to the front of her and holding the tail end of the string of feathers between finger and thumb, while he did his manful best to ignore how good she looked and smelled up close.

Her flowery perfume was intriguing—both adult and innocent at the same time.

Laura snatched the feathers out of his hand. "Thank you. I can take care of this." Her blue eyes regarded him with deep suspicion. "I *said*, I can manage the rest."

Nick wasn't thick. He knew when he was being told to make himself scarce, but for a moment or two he hovered there, mesmerised by the surprising beauty of Laura Goodman's bare shoulders—marble-white and perfect like the shoulders of a Grecian statue.

"Look, I know you do this kind of thing for a living," she huffed, waving the tip of her feathery garment at him, "but some of us have different value systems."

He shook his head in bewilderment. "What do you mean? What exactly do you *know* that I do for a living?"

"Just go inside and find Susie," she snapped. "Having you here was her idea."

Somehow, Nick was getting the impression that going inside and finding Susie was going to be even less helpful than standing on the footpath with this feathered enigma—this sheep in vixen's clothing.

He didn't really know very much about Rob's bride-to-be. His mate's romance had been recklessly whirlwind.

"Look, I'll turn my back while you fix your dress," he said. "But I'd like some clarification here. I want to know who you think I am and why the blazes you brought me here instead of to Rob's party?"

Before she answered, a woman's voice called from the front gate of the party house.

"Laura? Is that you? Have you brought Nick? The girls are getting impatient."

Tall, dark and model-thin, Susie Thomson was waving to them. Nick charged down the footpath towards her. "What's this all about, Susie? I'm supposed to be at Rob's."

She beamed at him and linked a slim arm through his. "Oh, no you're not. This is exactly where you're supposed to be. Everybody's waiting." Giggling a little, she began to drag him towards the noisy house.

It occurred to Nick as the babble of female voices grew louder that some guys would find being dragged into a house bursting at the seams with tipsy single women the equivalent of being handed heaven on a plate. But a sixth sense warned him that he wasn't in for any pleasant surprises tonight.

He thought about snatching his arm away from Susie's and bolting down the street. But then his common sense reasoned that he was worrying unduly.

After all, this woman was about to marry his best mate and he was to be best man at their wedding on Saturday. Any minute now, this whole confusing evening would begin to make sense.

Susie sent him another grin over her sequin-spangled shoulder as she pushed at her front door. "These girls can't wait," she laughed.

Then the door flew open and, just as he'd feared, Nick found himself facing a room filled with laughing, shouting women. They were all clutching champagne cocktails and were dressed in costumes so outrageous they made Laura Goodman's feathers look like the last word in good taste.

"Girls," Susie yelled, and the noise died down as their eyes swung Nick's way. "Our stripper is here at last!"

Strip—

Stripper!

At first Nick thought he was choking.

Then he was sure he was having a heart attack. He was drenched by a tidal wave of adrenaline. There was a roaring in his ears, which he realised later was the massed squeal of the women in front of him.

"You've got to be joking," he finally managed to croak.

Susie's grip on his arm tightened. "Of course this isn't a joke. Rob told me what a great party trick you do."

"Huh?" he wheezed. "*Rob* told you that?"

For several puzzled seconds he stared at Susie, but as panic squeezed every last molecule of air from his lungs the penny dropped. Rob Parker, his mate, had pulled a swift one.

He and Rob shared a long tradition of practical jokes and dares dating back to their primary school days in the bush and Nick recognised this as Rob's handiwork—the ultimate practical joke.

But he hadn't thought his friend was capable of such exceedingly poor taste. In the past, their dares had been risky, but never risqué!

Feeling just a little light-headed, he gritted his teeth in an attempt at a smile. "OK, Susie, you've frightened the life out of me. Well done. Neat trick. So what happens now? Rob's arranged for someone to take me to his party, hasn't he?"

"Not yet, Nick," Susie said sweetly but emphatically. "Not till the girls have had their show." Her brows drew together. "But I do have a message for you from Rob. He said you wouldn't *dare* to chicken out on us.''

''D—dare?'' he echoed.

''I reckon these girls will lynch you if you even think about leaving before you *perform*.''

Nick's throat felt so dry he was sure someone had lined it with sandpaper. This was the end of a perfect friendship.

Neither he nor Rob had ever refused a dare since they were eight years old when Nick had challenged his friend to run through a bull paddock. But when he found Rob, after this, his old mate would probably have to reconsider his wedding plans.

Nick looked again at Susie's determined face—at the gleeful expectation on the faces of the women pressing forward—and wondered briefly where Laura Goodman had got to. She'd be hiding and feeling very guilty, no doubt.

But he didn't have time to give her another thought as he accepted the terrible certainty that no one was planning to let him out of this dilemma.

His stomach knotted. "You're expecting me to strip?"

"Darlin'," Susie smiled silkily, "you know we are."

"Down to my jocks?"

Susie rolled her eyes as if she'd never heard such an inane question.

Frantically he looked around him. At the far end of the room stood a table laden with savouries. "I'll—I'll need some sustenance first."

"Of course!" Susie called to another woman, "Amanda, can you look after some food for our guest?"

There was a scattering of females and, within what seemed like seconds, half a dozen plates were thrust towards Nick. He took as long as he could, exchanging small talk and sampling the variety of foods eagerly offered by a circle of wide-eyed women.

"My, you eat so slowly," a sultry blonde purred. "I love a man who's not in a hurry."

He almost choked as he crammed more food into his mouth.

But a bloke could only consume so many Thai fish cakes, crudités, cheese, olives and Chinese chicken wings. He swilled down two champagne cocktails in quick succession, hoping he'd feel braver.

He didn't.

So he asked for another.

Susie appeared at his side and murmured, ''Ready?''

''I—I'm going to need special music for this. I can't just perform to any old tune.''

She smiled, ''I have a huge selection of CDs. Come and make your choice.''

In a frantic daze, Nick managed to spin out another five minutes as he sorted through Susie's collection, but all too soon she reached over and took the CD he held.

''Latin American. Good choice. This will be perfect.''

He felt a surge of panic. ''Oh—er—I'm not sure about that.''

''I am,'' she said sweetly but firmly. Then she slipped it into the player and turned to her guests. ''Girls, let's give a warm welcome to

Nick, who has something very special to show us!''

His head pounded as the room filled with ecstatic cheering and clapping.

CHAPTER TWO

LAURA took her time fixing her dress. She needed to stay in the darkened street and compose herself. When he'd offered to rearrange her feathers Nick Farrell had looked at her— the way a man looked at a woman when he found her—*desirable*. That wicked glint in his eye had been unmistakable.

And, to her utter embarrassment, instead of being repulsed, Laura had found his interest exciting.

How could she? The man was immoral. For pity's sake, he stripped for a living! But the really silly part was that a gleam in a man's eye was really nothing to get excited about.

He was only flirting. Right now he would be inside, sending each and every woman at the party a look so smouldering he would probably activate Susie's newly installed smoke alarms.

Pacing the footpath, she allowed the night air to fan her flaming cheeks and reminded herself that any of the other girls at this party would have responded to Nick's gaze with a flirtatious laugh. But she also knew she would never be like any other girl at this party.

She'd never really fitted in with her generation. Most of her friends saw her as twenty-nine going on fifty.

And that was how she was. She couldn't help it.

She was a Goodman.

From about the age of ten Laura had understood that her family was more earnest than most. The name Goodman had almost certainly been given to one of her ancestors because he had been exactly what it described— a *good* man. Since then, Goodman descendants had been both blessed and cursed with an over-supply of goodness genes.

Laura came from a long line of do-gooders.

In true Goodman tradition, she'd been born in a hut in Cambodia where her mother and father had worked as a doctor and nurse team tending orphans. Although they'd returned to

Australia when Laura and her brother started school, both her parents had continued working long hours in a range of charities in addition to their jobs at the Royal Brisbane hospital.

Now they were working in East Timor, and her brother, Phil, in his final year of medical studies, was clearly following in their worthy footsteps. But, although Laura admired her family, she couldn't live up to their standards. She had been the black sheep and had turned into a bookworm instead of a caring nurse or doctor.

When she'd announced she wanted to become a librarian her parents had swallowed their disappointment and consoled themselves that at least she hadn't wanted to be anything totally frivolous like a violinist or an archaeologist.

But, even though she'd been allowed to indulge in her passion for reading, those Goodman genes had caught up with Laura. Which was why she found herself reading stories to the children's ward at the local hospital every Wednesday.

On the other hand Susie, her fellow librarian, was convinced that good works meant hunting out the sexiest romance novels and keeping them under the counter for her favourite elderly ladies.

After ten minutes or so of pacing, Laura felt calmer. Checking once more that her feathers were firmly in place, she finally made her way inside to join the party. But when she saw Susie on the far side of the room talking to Nick, she chose to keep at a safe distance.

By the time she'd greeted one or two friends and helped herself to an orange juice *without* champagne, Nick was strolling slowly to the middle of a space that had been made for him.

The room pulsed with a sexy Latin American beat and most of the girls edged forward, clapping to its rhythm.

Laura gulped. So this was it—her first strip show.

As far as she could tell from her position against the far wall Nick looked calm, almost haughtily proud. He hardly seemed to notice the crowd of eager spectators pressing close. She guessed that keeping a mental distance from his audience was how a professional approached this kind of thing. No doubt looking bored was part of the act.

"Oh, my," drooled one of Susie's cousins. "I think I've just seen my future—my perfect match. Do you think when his eyes reach mine across this crowded room he'll realise we're made for each other?"

"Dream on, Sandy," another girl scoffed.

The bold, throbbing music filled the room and Laura noticed that Nick was beginning to move to its rhythm. Turning his back to the audience, he strutted in an essentially masculine way, shifting first one whole side of his body then the other. The girls roared as he swivelled his hips in a manoeuvre that made his jeans stretch tight across his neat backside.

Someone groaned, "What a god!"

Laura had to admit he was good at this. The girls were loving it. Now his T-shirt was hanging loose out of his jeans and, as he turned to face them once more, he slowly lifted the white cotton knit to reveal a tempting glimpse of tanned torso with an arrowing of dark hair disappearing into his jeans.

There were calls of, "Get it off!"

Laura gulped. She was shocked by how difficult she found it to drag her eyes away from those few inches of masculine flesh.

In front of her, Sandy was swooning. "You can tell he'd be good in bed just by the way he moves," she sighed.

The girls drooled in unison as Nick lifted the T-shirt higher.

Laura took an extra long sip of orange juice and her drink finished in a noisy slurp. She was beginning to feel hot and flustered again. It was a long time since she'd really paid close attention to a man, especially a man removing his clothes, and she had to admit Nick Farrell looked good.

OK make that very, *very* good. But how could these women think about jumping straight into bed with a strange man just because they liked his appearance?

She scanned the sea of eager faces. It seemed everyone at the party liked the way Nick looked.

His shirt was off now and he was swinging it over his head in big, lazy circles. Of course, his chest and shoulders were as broad as Laura had suspected when she first saw him in the mall. She wondered if his skin would feel as amazing as it looked—like bronzed silk tightly stretched over hard, man-sized muscles.

Shocked by her totally improper interest, Laura dragged her eyes upwards, away from his body, and to her dismay she found Nick's eyes meeting with hers. From across the room they sparkled cheekily as he winked at her.

How dared he?

Instinctively, Laura sent back an icy glare— the sort that usually silenced the rowdiest patrons in her library—but he simply grinned and winked some more.

In one synchronised flowing movement, the heads of the women in the room swung round to see who was attracting so much attention.

Laura felt her cheeks flame. There was a buzz of feminine reaction, the unpleasant sound of catty whispers. She dropped her gaze and stabbed at the bottom of her empty juice glass with her straw. Why did this bare-chested moron have to embarrass her like this?

Nick was despicable. She'd done nothing to deserve such singling out. Embarrassed, she hurried towards the front door, but, as she did so, she saw out of the corner of her eye that Nick was tossing his T-shirt to a pretty brunette in the centre of the room.

An excited squeal erupted and she couldn't believe the little spurt of disappointment she felt. What the dickens was wrong with her? Of course she was relieved that he'd turned his attention to another woman.

This was too much! For one scary minute she'd been eyeing Nick Farrell with as much lusty interest as the rest of the girls. Thank heavens she'd come to her senses when he gave her that indecent wink.

Safely outside on the patio once more, she leaned against the front wall of Susie's house and dragged in deep draughts of air, fighting for the second time that night to regain her composure.

A loud uproar exploded inside. No doubt Nick was nearing the climax of his act.

Laura closed her eyes and refused to imagine the scene on the other side of the wall.

Thank goodness she'd left the room when she had. It would have been far too embarrassing to have witnessed the final unveiling.

How could anyone—how could *Nick* do this sort of thing for a living just because he had a great body?

Nick had kept telling himself that at any minute Rob would appear to let him off the hook. But now he was beginning to fear there'd be no reprieve. With his shirt off and his belt already gone, he was facing his darkest hour. His hands actually shook as he fingered the metal button at the top of his jeans.

The wide-eyed females before him were grinning stupidly.

"Don't worry about leaving your jeans lying on the floor, sweetheart, I'll pick them up later," someone called.

And it was about then that Nick Farrell knew he'd hit a brick wall.

There was no way he would take this charade to the bitter end. There was no way in Christendom this best man was going to show his mate's bride exactly who was the *best* man.

He let his hands drop loosely to his sides and stood still.

Perched on a stool at the side of the room, Susie was watching him carefully.

Nick shook his head at her.

Her eyebrow arched in a silent question.

''Show's over,'' he mouthed.

In reply, a grim-mouthed, very determined Susie shook her head.

A film of sweat broke out on Nick's forehead. For the life of him he couldn't remember what kind of jocks he'd dragged on tonight. He inched the zipper of his jeans down a little and was relieved to glimpse solid black cotton.

OK—he'd go down to his jocks, but that was definitely the end of the line. Susie had threatened lynching. Well—that would be a character-building experience.

Nervously, he stepped out of his jeans. He knew he'd stopped performing, but, strangely, it didn't seem to matter. The room filled with even louder cheers and enthusiastic clapping. Anyone would think this was the Olympics and he'd broken a world record.

Susie was grinning and walking towards him. That grin would be wiped in a flash when he told her this was it. The finish line.

The end.

Feeling foolish, Nick stood there, holding his jeans in front of him. Susie continued to grin and clap. The whole room filled with applause.

"This is absolutely as far as I go," he warned her.

She nodded. "I know."

"You *know?*"

"Of course. You've got to turn up at church for my wedding on Saturday and most of these women will be there. We have to maintain some decorum. Besides, we can't ruin your fine reputation as Crown Prosecutor, can we?"

Nick stared at her as he felt the room sway. "So this *was* a set-up? Rob's idea?"

Susie shrugged and her lips curved in a sly smile. "You'd better ask him about that."

"These women—did they know I'm not a stripper? They weren't expecting..."

"They knew the score, but I hope you'll forgive us. You were fantastic. You're a hero, Nick."

Feeling anything but heroic, Nick clambered back into his jeans. He'd been taken for a ride by his best mate and a bunch of giggling females. This wasn't the first time he'd been at the wrong end of a practical joke and it probably wouldn't be the last, but it was taking longer than usual for him to catch on to the humour.

As he threaded his belt back through the loops of his jeans, he asked, "Laura Goodman knew I was being conned?"

"Laura?" Susie frowned.

"The chauffeur. The feather duster with the Titian hair and the long legs."

Susie smiled. "I'm glad you noticed Laura's legs. She's sweet, isn't she?"

Nick grunted and wondered why on earth he *had* mentioned Laura Goodman or her legs.

"Actually," Susie said slowly, "I didn't explain to Laura exactly what was going on. So you mustn't be mad at her. She's going to be your—"

"It's not an issue," Nick interrupted, not wanting to dwell on the matter. "I want out of here. I'll grab a cab to Rob's party. I've got a bone to pick with my humorous mate."

Suddenly serious, Susie pleaded, "Be nice to him, please, Nick. This really was just a little fun. He said you both play jokes on each other."

She stood on tiptoe and lightly kissed his cheek. "And thanks so much for being a sport about it all. You were terrific."

"Just get me back my T-shirt and I'll think about how nice I'm going to be."

From the safety of the patio, Laura guessed that the strip show was over. The party seemed to have quietened considerably. She glanced at her watch and decided to pop inside and speak to Susie, then make her excuses before slipping away. Susie would understand her hasty departure when she explained about tomorrow's clown problem.

But the doorway was blocked by a tall, dark, bare-chested figure. Nick Farrell was coming out, dragging a T-shirt over his head.

"Oh," she said as his face emerged, "it's you." She lifted her chin, but it was hard to look down her nose at someone so much taller. "I suppose you want a lift back, do you?"

"No," he scowled. "I'll get a cab."

"I'm supposed to be your chauffeur," Laura said quickly. And then she could have kicked herself. Why on earth had she been so eager to help him?

Tucking his shirt into his jeans, Nick cocked his head to one side and studied her. He smiled slowly. "You'll take me to the groom's party this time?"

She couldn't help showing her horror. "You're not going to strip for the men, too?"

He took an age to reply. Eventually, she heard a soft chuckle. "You really do have a very low opinion of me, don't you?"

His words sent a wave of remorse coursing through her. Perhaps that chuckle was his way of covering hurt feelings. She must have sounded very judgemental. "I'm sorry. What you do is really none of my business."

Nick's mouth twitched as if he was having difficulty controlling his reaction and Laura was quite sure she had hurt him.

Beneath the bold and brassy body, he was almost certainly hiding a sensitive soul. She'd been thinking all evening how terrible it was that such a fit, well-spoken and intelligent-looking man had been reduced to taking off his clothes to make a living.

There was a red tinge staining his neck and cheekbones and the realisation that she had embarrassed Nick was enough to activate an entire battalion of Laura's do-good genes.

Suddenly she saw the chance to do something really special. It was obvious that Nick needed help. With some tactful pressure, she could encourage him to raise his sights and find a proper job. She could even save him from further degradation.

In a flash, she decided that tomorrow would be soon enough to explain to Susie why she'd left the party so quickly. "Hop into my car," she ordered in a businesslike manner and, to her relief, he obeyed without further argument.

By the time they were halfway to Rob's party she had figured out a brilliant plan for launching Nick Farrell's rehabilitation. "You know, you have very fine entertainment skills," she began in her warmest manner.

Sounding mildly surprised, he muttered his thanks.

"Have you ever thought about using those skills for different kinds of entertainment?"

"Different?" In her peripheral vision, Laura was aware of the way Nick's big shoulders rolled as he turned to look at her. "How different do you mean?"

She swallowed and, for a moment, concentrated on taking a sharp corner. "There are nobler ways of entertaining people that could earn you just as much money," she suggested gently. "Well, maybe I should amend that—almost as much money. I'm sure stripping does pay very well, but—"

They came to a stop sign and Laura stole a glance at Nick to see how he was taking this. She was dismayed to see that he was looking very uncomfortable. "Oh, dear," she whispered.

She'd hurt him again. Maybe her mother was right. She should have taken that evening course in counselling. He'd covered his face with his hands and was taking deep breaths. She thought she heard something like a hiccup.

Laura felt terrible.

But then, when Nick lowered his hands again, he looked at her very seriously and said, "Exactly what kind of work are you suggesting?"

Laura beamed. "I could find you a good job in no time. In fact I can organise a job tomorrow as a clown at the children's hospital. I'd pay you award rates."

She didn't quite catch his reaction. The traffic had cleared and she had to keep her eyes on the road as she accelerated across the intersection, but, as soon as she could, she looked his way. "What do you think?"

"A job as a clown? I'm stunned."

"You'd make a great clown," she urged, hoping he couldn't guess that she actually needed him to do this job as much as he needed the work.

"I'm not sure that I'm flattered."

"But you'd feel so good knowing you've brightened the day for all those little kids."

"As a *clown?*"

"You'd be using your talents for something truly worthwhile."

He frowned. "Will you be there?"

Laura pulled to a stop outside his destination, the Royal Hotel. "Yes, I'll be there, Nick," she said in her most reassuring voice. "I'm going to read a couple of stories to the children. I'll provide you with a costume. You just have to improvise and clown around—like you did tonight—sort of."

When he hesitated, she added, "Go on. I dare you to try it just once."

"You *dare* me?" he repeated. His hand was on the door handle and Laura could tell he was eager to go.

"Yes," she replied boldly. "Do you accept dares?"

He turned to her with a smile so slow and sexy it sizzled the blood in her veins. "OK, I'll dare to do this Beppo the clown stunt if you dare to give this big bad stripper a kiss."

CHAPTER THREE

ASKING for the kiss was stupid, but the words had spilled out before Nick had time to rein in his wayward thoughts.

For most of the drive across town he had been hard-pressed to keep a straight face while Laura Goodman sat there sounding and acting as prissy and prim as a Sunday School teacher bent on saving his soul. She behaved as if she had no idea that her body looked sinfully sexy in those feathers.

But even if she didn't know who he was, and still thought he was a professional stripper, how could any woman with hair that rich red colour and eyes such an astonishing blue behave as if she'd never been asked for a kiss before?

What a reaction! Shock! Horror! Scandalised big blue eyes. The message was clear. Laura Goodman couldn't bring herself

44

to kiss Nick Farrell if he was the last man on the planet.

The princess couldn't kiss the frog.

That was fine, Nick decided. A big relief! Kissing a woman who took herself as seriously as Laura would be dangerous. It had been a crazy proposition to put to her and now he had a nice simple reason to escape her ridiculous clown gig without going into complicated explanations.

He reached once more for the door handle.

''Nick.'' Laura's voice was just a little squeaky.

''Yeah?''

''I can understand why you asked me for the kiss. I guess you see it as a fair deal.'' The tip of her pink tongue made a sexy little circuit around her lips.

''Ah—a spur-of-the-moment suggestion,'' he mumbled. ''Forget it.''

''No!'' she cried with a sudden urgency that startled him. Then she startled him some more by leaning closer and continuing earnestly. ''I want you to do the clown job, so I'll kiss you.

But…'' She didn't seem to know how to finish the sentence.

And Nick was too stupefied to think of anything to say.

Seconds later, Laura edged closer, bringing again that hint of roses and jasmine—like the first hot day of spring. ''I'm not exactly in the habit of kissing men I've just met,'' she murmured more than a touch nervously.

Out of the corner of his eye, he saw her pause and stare at him as if she were summoning up strength and he waited for her excuse to escape from this tiresome task.

''You'd make it easier for me if you could turn your head this way,'' she said huskily.

Get out of this car, Nick told himself, but he stayed, convinced the woman held a postgraduate degree in seduction. Her apparent inexperience, her bossiness and her beauty were an intoxicating mix. He'd never felt such sudden *heat*.

It was on the tip of his tongue to say, *It's OK. You don't have to do this. It was a bad idea.* But he was already turning his head her

way and she was lifting her soft, lush lips towards his.

Her skin was exquisitely clear and pale, an
intriguing contrast to her vibrant hair.
Strawberries and cream. He had to taste her.

Her mouth touched briefly against his lower
lip and sent desire flaring and shuddering
through his body.

She made a soft, apologetic sound. "I
wasn't quite close enough," she whispered.
"I'll try again."

Oh, yes! In a kind of blissful agony, Nick
closed his eyes and this time Laura's lips settled firmly, softly, warmly against his. He
tasted their sweetness and then he heard her
rapid breathing, felt her hands on the sides of
his face, sensed her lips opening beneath his.

And there was only one thing a fellow could
do. He kissed her back.

It was only meant to be a gentle kiss. After
all, this prudish little creature was easily
shocked. But her mouth was so unexpectedly
warm and welcoming and before he had time
to reconsider, Nick's lips and tongue became

fused in a hungry, urgent, dizzying tangle with Laura's.

And incredibly, instead of protesting, she made soft little needy sounds. Sounds that begged him for more. Sounds that drove him crazy.

He *was* crazy. He shouldn't be doing this. Not with her.

But her hands were roaming restlessly over his shoulders and her mouth was moving against his with increasing eagerness. This wasn't the time to question his sanity.

It was time to slip his fingers into her silky hair and discover if it felt as good as it looked. Damn, it felt even better. Soft. So soft. Her coppery curls wrapped themselves around his fingers. And he wanted all of her wrapped around him.

Nick couldn't remember a kiss that had sent him so wild so fast. He needed to haul her closer, to feel all of her soft curves pressed under him, to peel away those feathers.

Don't touch the feathers!

He jerked his hands away from Laura's temptingly bare shoulders as if they were glowing hot embers. And the action was enough to jolt both of them back into reality. To the reality that they were still in her car and parked in a busy suburban street outside a pub full of his mates.

They were both a touch breathless. Nick was more than a little shell-shocked. He figured Laura felt the same way. But he was damned sure he wasn't going to apologise for kissing her. Best not to discuss that kiss at all.

"Well," he managed to say at last, "I'd say you won that dare, so you'd better tell me where to line up for this job tomorrow morning."

With cheeks of bright pink, Laura resumed her place in the driver's seat, took a deep breath and hooked a fiery curl behind one ear. "Could you meet me at nine-thirty at the Casey Street entrance to the Glenwood hospital?" she asked so politely she might have been issuing an invitation to dine with the Queen.

Nick nodded. Heaven help him. He had the softest heart in the country. Or was that the softest head? First a strip show, now a clown act. Twice in one night he'd let himself be conned into doing something he didn't want to do.

But he could hardly wriggle out of this agreement after Little Miss Prim had so bravely sacrificed her mouth and her high moral standards for the sake of a ward full of sick kids.

He wasn't due in court until eleven tomorrow.

"It's a done deal," he told her. "Thanks for the—er—lift." And, opening the car door, Nick dived into the pub before he could change his mind.

About anything.

"You're looking happy." Susie looked up from the pile of returned books she was processing to greet Laura. "I take it the hospital session went well this morning?"

Laura hadn't realised she was wearing such a wide grin. She reassembled her features into something more sober. "It went really well," she agreed. "The children loved it. Nick was brilliant. He's even more athletic than I realised. He can do handstands and he can juggle—well, he can almost juggle. Thank goodness he was only using oranges. He can—''

''Hey, hold it!?'' Susie interrupted. ''Did you say Nick?''

''Nick Farrell, the hit of your party last night. I've encouraged him to extend his repertoire.''

Susie blinked and gulped in a very fair imitation of a stunned mullet. ''But don't you have someone regular that you use for your hospital work?''

Laura smiled. ''I didn't have time to tell you last night, but Moe's come down with a virus and he couldn't make it. Luckily, it wasn't a problem. I talked Nick Farrell into standing in for him. He was a brilliant clown.''

The six books Susie had been holding thumped onto the counter top. ''He was *what?*'' People reading nearby looked up and frowned at them. She stepped closer to Laura and asked her again in a quieter, but distinctly strained, voice, ''You got *Nick Farrell* to be a clown?''

"Yes," Laura said defensively. "I don't see why you should look so shocked. You hired him to strip butt naked. I simply hired him to put those same entertaining skills to a better purpose. He really brightened the day for those sick kids."

Susie was spluttering. "But—but how on earth did you persuade him to do it?"

An elderly couple arrived at the counter to check out their books and, grateful for the excuse to avoid answering Susie's question, Laura turned away quickly to serve them. There was no way she would go into the precise details of exactly how she'd persuaded Nick to help her.

Not that she really believed that kiss had been a deciding factor for him. But she was doing her darned best to delete all thoughts of it. If she tried to analyse just how that kiss had happened her mind went into meltdown mode. She hadn't just kissed the man, she'd practically eaten him alive.

Laura Do-good had lost her head in an outburst of uncontrolled lust with a professional strip-tease artist!

She'd only been able to face Nick this morning because he'd been so well disguised behind clown's paint, a curly red wig, stripy pants and long-toed shoes.

But Susie wasn't to be put off. As soon as there was a lull at the desk, she was beside Laura, brimming with questions. "I just can't believe you got Nick to do that clown gig," she began. "I mean, to start with, how did he get time away from court?"

"Court?" Laura echoed faintly. The walls of the library seemed to close in suddenly. She felt dizzy. "He—he's on trial?" Had she hurled herself into the arms of a criminal?

"No. Of course he's not on trial, silly." Susie stared hard at Laura. "Oh, my goodness," she whispered. "You don't know... Who do you think...? You don't think Nick was—a *real* stripper, do you?"

"Of course he's a real stripper. How much more real do you want? The man took all his clothes off in a room full of women!"

Again, the heads from the reading corner jerked in their direction. There were a few eyebrows raised and knowing smirks exchanged.

Laura flinched.

"Gee, Laura, I'm sorry I didn't fill you in on the plan," Susie replied *sotto voce*. "I guess I was worried you mightn't like it." She bent her head closer and outlined in clear and certain terms the exact circumstances that had led to Nick's appearance at her party—how she'd stopped him just short of baring his prime exhibits *and* exactly how he filled in most of his days in court.

"Crown Prosecutor!" Laura squeaked as she clung to the counter for support. "You mean to tell me I wasted good sleeping time last night planning ways to keep that man from the depths of moral depravity and he spends his days being a pillar of society—an upholder of law and justice?"

"'Fraid so." Susie nodded, and grimaced.

Laura stifled a shriek. This was not a good moment to be in a library. She'd made an A-class fool of herself. And Nick Farrell had let her. He'd *helped* her make a fool of herself.

This morning she'd paid him twenty-four dollars for his hour's work—and she'd impressed on him that it was six dollars over the award. And the creep had acted as if she'd done him a big favour when, chances were, he pulled in thousands of dollars in a day!

Dimly, Laura realised that Susie was still talking. "Anyhow, you have to admit Nick's ultra-cute, isn't he?"

To her horror, Laura felt a bright red blush sweep up her neck and cheeks till it reached the roots of her crimson hair. "No way," she protested with unnecessary vehemence. "He's got nothing going for him."

Just the sexiest mouth in the Southern hemisphere.

Susie grinned. "You didn't notice his body? His face? His cheeky smile?"

"He's definitely not my type," Laura sniffed. *And wasn't that the honest truth?* The man was an exhibitionist and a sneaky fake. But she knew her denial sounded weak and feeble when her red face was making such an eloquent statement.

"That's a pity," murmured Susie with a sly smile.

Laura didn't want to ask, but she couldn't help herself. "Why do you say that?"

''Because you're going to have to see each other again on Saturday.''

''Don't tell me he's coming to the wedding?''

''He sure is. If Rob and I hadn't decided to get married in such a crazy rush I guess you would have met him at an engagement party or something, but Nick's going to be Rob's best man. Which means, my dear, that he'll be your partner.''

G-r-r-reat! Laura spun away abruptly and bit down on an explosive retort. *This couldn't be happening!* Grabbing an armful of books, she stacked them onto the return trolley in completely the wrong order while she wondered desperately if it would be terribly bad form to beg Susie to demote her from her position as bridesmaid.

How could she face Nick Farrell? She'd been hoping she'd never have to set eyes on the man again for the rest of her days. Meeting him had been the start of a series of disasters. She'd made one gigantic mistake after another!

First there'd been the prudish sermons about how he could better himself, then she'd locked her lips with him like a sex-starved loser. And now, this morning, she'd paid him peanuts to be a circus clown.

She tried to look and sound calm. "Nick's the best man? That's fine. It's a simple job. We'll hardly have to do anything together except follow you down the aisle. I'll—I'll be busy keeping your veil and train in order and he'll be totally preoccupied propping up Rob."

Susie picked up one of the books Laura had misplaced and slotted it into its correct position on the trolley.

"We'll see," she murmured. And to Laura's embarrassment, her friend's finger gently traced her flushed cheek. "But there are some interesting symptoms showing here. If you don't have the hots for Nick Farrell, I'm wondering why you're redder than the proverbial beetroot."

Everything about weddings was designed to make a man nervous, Nick decided as he took his place beside Rob the following Saturday. The hired suits, the unfamiliar music played on a wheezy organ, the damp-eyed relatives in the front pews and the silent, expectant hush of the rest of the congregation.

It was all a far cry from the rollicking, boozy fun of the bucks' party a few nights ago.

Rob was restless as he waited for Susie to appear. "Have you got the rings?" he muttered.

Nick frowned. "What rings?"

Rob's face blanched. "I gave them to you last night. Remember?"

"Are you sure you did?" Nick patted his coat pockets and then checked the deeper pockets in his trousers.

"Oh, my God!" Rob stared at Nick and then sank his head into his hands. "I don't believe it. This can't happen. Not now!" He looked completely shaken, on the point of nervous collapse.

With the fingers of his right hand, Nick felt his fob pocket again. "Oh," he said, withdrawing two golden circles. "You mean these rings?"

Rob's head shot up. "You rat!"

For an uncomfortable second or two the two mates eyed each other. Then a corner of Nick's mouth twitched and Rob's mouth curled in answer.

Rob shook his head and his eyes sparkled knowingly. ''I knew you'd find a way to get me back for that surprise gig at Susie's party.''

''Too right,'' Nick answered with a grin.

''Er—hem—gentlemen—'' The vicar leaned towards them. ''The bridal party has arrived.''

Suddenly the organ launched into the dramatic opening chords of Mendelssohn's ''Wedding March.''

''Here she comes.'' Rob swung around eagerly to face the back of the church. Nick followed, wishing he didn't have to feel so choked up.

He wasn't worried that Rob was going to his doom. He was happy for the guy. Rob was head over heels in love with Susie and there was nothing to—

Hold on! Nick's meditation on his mate's future was arrested by the scene at the end of the flower-decked aisle. Susie was there, framed in a stone archway, looking bridal and lovely in white and smiling broadly.

But just in front of her was a redhead in blue.

That redhead in blue.

Something alarming happened to Nick's chest and his ability to breathe. For a second or two, there seemed to be only one woman in the church. Laura Goodman. She was moving slowly towards him, her amazing blue feathers replaced by something floaty and elegant in a paler blue.

Nick squared his shoulders and blinked. She was still there. This wasn't part of last night's dream. She was still moving slowly forward, carrying a mass of delicate blossoms. Her vibrant hair was caught at the sides of her head in clusters of tiny flowers, but from there it fell away in loose waves that shone like dark flames against her pale, perfect shoulders.

A short strand of pearls gleamed at her creamy throat. The woman was beautiful! Her deep blue eyes glowed softly with a powerful emotion. But they were fixed straight ahead of her as she preceded Susie down the aisle.

Not once did they stray in Nick's direction.

He told himself he was glad that she wasn't looking at him. He was relieved that she didn't make any kind of eye contact as she reached the chancel steps and stood to one side to make room for the bride.

In fact it would be best if they both acted as if they hardly knew each other. Dear God, they *did* hardly know one another.

And yet, despite their brief and vexing acquaintance, this uptight librarian had kissed him with a fire that had practically launched him into orbit. The impact of that kiss had stayed with Nick ever since.

By heaven, Laura's kiss had been hotter than a midsummer's night. She tasted sweeter than the freshest spring morning. Sexier than anything he'd experienced in years. He'd found getting out of her car one of the hardest exits he'd ever made.

On the strength of that kiss, his dreams had been X-rated for several nights in a row. But just how that astonishing encounter had happened so unexpectedly would probably remain one of the unsolved mysteries of the new millennium.

Of course he'd paid for it with that crazy clown caper the next morning...

The vicar moved forward and, with a start, Nick realised the man was addressing the congregation. "Dearly beloved..."

He dragged his focus back to the job at hand. Rob and Susie's wedding day. The start of thirty, forty, who knew how many years of matrimonial bliss. Nice if you could get it. He wished them well.

He hadn't been too lucky.

But his own marriage was the last thing Nick wanted to think about today. That was territory too painful to visit.

Laura thought she was doing well. If she could keep herself mentally distanced from Nick Farrell she would be able to maintain her composure throughout the wedding ceremony.

She concentrated on Susie. In her slim-fitting satin gown and dreamy veil, her friend looked radiant and beautiful. The perfect bride. On the other side of her stood Rob. She'd never seen a guy look so happy and eager to tie the knot.

In fact Rob's happiness, his love for Susie and his quiet confidence, seemed to spread a calming aura over the whole wedding party. Laura remained aware of Nick, tall and dark and well, yes, she couldn't deny it—impossibly handsome—on the far side of the more solid Rob, but as the beautiful ceremony progressed his presence became less disturbing.

The hymns were sung, the vows and rings exchanged and blessings given, and she gradually relaxed and allowed herself to become totally absorbed in Susie's happiness.

But her serenity evaporated when it was time to follow the ecstatic couple back down the aisle. Then everything came back to her. Every embarrassing reason why she should turn tail and flee.

Nick had already stepped forward to take the place Rob vacated and he stood facing her with his elbow cocked, waiting for her to link her arm with his. Unfair! He was too tall and dark to ignore. Too dashingly handsome in his formal suit. Too darned good-looking to forget what it felt like to—

Stop it! Laura lifted her head haughtily, and with the faintest smile and minimum eye contact, allowed Nick to take her arm. Beneath the smooth sleeve of his jacket she could feel the solid muscle of his forearm, but she focused her eyes ahead on Susie's veil, making sure it was trailing neatly behind her. She smiled at the rows of beaming faces.

Nick murmured, "Good afternoon, Laura," in his deep, resonant voice and she dipped her head to acknowledge his greeting, but didn't look his way.

The one thing she didn't want to do was blush. With her pale complexion, a blush was like wearing a sign on her forehead that read: Foolish Flustered Female. But trying not to go red meant not looking at Nick, not thinking about him or the ridiculous mistakes she'd made, and not getting angry with him for stringing her along.

It was a tall order.

Progress out of the church was slow because Susie and Rob kept stopping to be congratulated and hugged by relatives and friends, but with three-quarters of the aisle covered Laura began to breathe more easily. A few more steps and they would be outside. Then she could mingle and mix with the crowd and this *togetherness* part of the ordeal would be over.

Towards the back of the church two adorable little girls were leaning forward, almost falling out of their pew as they grinned and waved madly. Laura guessed they were sisters. Although they didn't look alike, they were wearing identical dark green dresses with white lace collars and cuffs.

She smiled at them and their faces lit up, their eyes rounded with excitement. To her surprise, she realised they were looking at Nick and herself with the kind of adoration and awe that was usually reserved for the very famous. She heard Nick's soft chuckle and turned to see that he was grinning at the girls.

Her heart gave a funny little jump as she saw the way his deep grey eyes glowed when he smiled at them.

"Aren't they sweet?" she couldn't help commenting.

"Most of the time," came his surprising answer.

Then suddenly the smaller girl, a rosy-cheeked moppet with glossy dark curls, slipped out of her seat and into the aisle in front of them. "Daddy!" she called excitedly, looking straight up at Nick.

"Daddy?" Laura squeaked.

This irresponsible jester was a father?

She reached for the end of a pew to support her shaky legs. *She'd exchanged passionate kisses with a married man? No, she couldn't have. Not again!*

CHAPTER FOUR

NICK watched as Laura's shocked gaze darted from his daughter to himself and back again. He knew his little girl's features were diminutive, feminine versions of his own thick, dark hair, distinctive nose and steel grey eyes. No DNA testing required to determine this paternity issue.

Bending down, he picked up the cuddly bundle in an easy, familiar movement and he dropped a happy kiss on her warm cheek. She beamed with delight. ''This is Fliss,'' he told Laura. ''My number-two daughter.''

''My proper name's Felicity,'' the child corrected in her usual bossy manner, taking care to pronounce her name very carefully.

Laura's blue eyes clouded and Nick couldn't tell if she was stunned or angry or both. She looked as if she was suffering from severe shock, but perhaps she was just being a female—and feeling soppy about Susie's wedding.

His older daughter stepped forward. ''And this is Kate,'' he explained, ''my big girl.''

He didn't feel ready to explain at this moment that the reason Kate's hair was as fine and pale as Felicity's was thick and dark was because she took after her mother.

Laura seemed to have trouble responding to Kate's shy smile, but at last she managed to speak. ''Hello, Kate—and Felicity.'' Her stunned gaze swung to the grey-haired woman who'd been standing with the girls.

''And this is Heather Cunningham, my mother-in-law.''

The two women exchanged polite greetings. ''I've seen you before—at the Glenwood library,'' the older woman added.

''Heather brought the girls to the church to see the wedding, but they won't be attending the reception,'' Nick explained.

''Uhhuh,'' was the only answer Laura seemed capable of making.

But his daughters weren't so tongue-tied.

"I love your dress," Kate said, gazing up at Laura as if she were a fairy tale princess come to life. "And your flowers."

Not to be outdone, Felicity tightened her plump arms around his neck as she squeezed him in an excited hug. "Daddy," she cried, "I like your pretty lady. Are you going to get married, too?"

Before he could react to Felicity's question, Nick heard a helpless, choking sound beside him. Laura looked paler and more shocked than ever.

"Do you need to sit down?" he asked her.

She shook her head.

It occurred to him that she was probably feeling sorry for these poor children, who had a degenerate stripper for a father; she could even be wondering where their mother was.

Desperately, he tried to think of a simple way to explain his situation without upsetting anyone present. In court, he was famous for his sharp mind and quick, precise verbal responses.

But talking about this was different.

This was about Miranda.

There were actual tears in Laura's blue eyes. Her mouth quivered. And damn it, Nick wanted to cry, too. Eight years ago he'd been married, just as Rob had today. He'd been incredibly young, but filled to overflowing with love for his bride. He should still be married now!

He blinked and tried to distract his thoughts by rubbing his nose against Felicity's.

''Daddy?'' the little girl persisted. ''Didn't you hear me? I've got a really good idea. You can marry this pretty lady.''

Nick almost dropped his daughter. ''Not today, Fliss,'' he hedged, only just managing to keep his voice steady. ''It's Rob's turn to get married today.'' He shot Laura an apologetic grimace.

''You've quite captivated the girls, Laura,'' Heather Cunningham said with a cautious smile that didn't quite reach her eyes.

Nick realised his mother-in-law was right. Here was Fliss, innocently demanding that he marry the pretty bridesmaid, while Kate was standing as close as possible to Laura and looking up at her with huge brown eyes. Kate usually only looked at stray kittens with that much depth of feeling.

He'd never seen his elder daughter so impressed by anyone. If he wasn't careful the girls would start a Laura Goodman fan club, right here on the church steps.

He had to admit that Laura was looking exceptionally beautiful today with her glowing hair loosely framing her delicate face. And her gown was all filmy and feminine, the sort of romantic get-up that all little girls probably dreamed of wearing one day.

It was a pity his daughters hadn't met Laura at her library, with her fiery hair scraped back into a neat, no-nonsense knot and her feminine curves disguised by a serviceable navy shirt dress—the way she'd looked at the hospital the other day. Then the girls wouldn't have been nearly so impressed by her and there would have been no embarrassing comments.

He suggested to Heather that it was time to take Kate and Felicity home.

"Not yet!" they protested, but Nick remained firm.

"I'll give your daddy my bouquet to bring home," Laura promised the girls, and after that they went away quite happily with their grandmother, but not until both Nick and Laura had submitted to hugs and kisses.

As Nick waved the girls off Laura turned to him, her eyes shining—no, not exactly shining, he realised with mild alarm, but rather shimmering. With emotion. Negative emotion. She was angry.

"I can't believe those dear little girls are your daughters," she hissed out of the side of her mouth.

He shrugged. "I guess it does take a fair stretch of the imagination."

"They're just so sweet," she added. "They're *gorgeous*."

"Amazing, isn't it?"

"They deserve a father who takes his responsibility seriously."

"Fair go," he protested. "I admit I'm not Father of the Year, but I'm not exactly a slack parent."

"But your morals are questionable."

"My morals?" He scowled at her.

She leaned close and whispered, ''Maybe you aren't a strip-tease artist.'' Her tone grew chilly as she added, ''And while we're on the subject, I didn't appreciate being strung along about that.''

He dug his hands into his coat pockets and felt his jaw stiffen.

''But,'' she continued, ''you can't pretend you don't know what I'm upset about now.''

Nick looked around him. Luckily all eyes were on the bride and groom. Rob and Susie were posing for photos on the church steps. ''No pretence,'' he told Laura. ''I'm dead serious. I don't know what you're talking about.''

''You persuaded me to kiss you.''

''That's immoral? A simple kiss?'' He looked around him again, worried that this ridiculous conversation might be overheard.

''It wasn't exactly a *simple* kiss,'' Laura muttered. ''A kiss on the cheek is simple.''

''Hey, let's not get tangled up in definitions.''

''And don't you play fancy lawyer games with me. Any kind of kiss—and you know the kind of kiss I'm talking about—should be saved for your wife.''

''My wife,'' Nick echoed softly, and he felt the strangeness of those words on his lips.

''I'm assuming you had enough moral fibre to marry the girls' mother.''

''Oh, yes,'' Nick said with a sigh. He could see the blue fire burning in Laura's eyes as she gathered steam for another barrage of questions. He decided to nip them in the bud.

''She's dead.''

''*What?*'' she whispered.

''My wife died.''

''Oh!'' Laura looked stricken. She covered her mouth with a shaking hand. ''Oh, Nick. I'm so sorry.''

''It's OK. It happened some time back. Fliss was only a baby.''

The very last thing Nick wanted was for Laura to go on saying how sorry she was. She didn't need to. He could see the remorse in her eyes. She had such an open, expressive face, it was as easy to read as a billboard.

''Those poor little girls.''

He suppressed a new surge of dismay. He'd seen that dreamy, sentimental look in the eyes of many women over the past five years when they'd discovered he was a widower. It was a look that set off alarm bells.

In the past, similar comments had always been followed up eventually, one way or another, by the message, *I'd just love to mother your daughters for you.*

And, given Laura Goodman's fondness for doing good deeds, chances were she would be simply bursting with willingness to take his daughters under her wing—just as she did those children at the hospital. But he certainly didn't want another wife and his girls didn't need another mother.

He, Kate and Felicity would go on managing just fine on their own.

However, he thought, with a self-mocking smile, it was a damn pity that Laura was so addicted to *morality* and *good* deeds. Didn't she realise that with her fiery hair and blazing blue eyes, not to mention her sexy hot mouth and slim curves, she'd been designed for bad,

bad deeds...*wicked* deeds...?

But that was a different story altogether.

Laura felt an unpleasant dizzy sensation when she joined Susie and Rob for photos in front of the church. It was as if she'd stepped off one of those scary rides at a sideshow.

At first, when she'd discovered Nick was a father, her response had been a nauseating flood of ghastly, guilty memories. Memories of the affair she'd had with Oliver before she'd found out about his wife and boys.

Five years ago she'd suffered so much guilt she'd actually made herself ill. She still felt sickened whenever she thought about Oliver's family.

After Oliver's shocking confession, she'd been so desperate for proof that she'd tracked down his home address and spied on them. She'd seen his wife drive the boys home from school, watched them laughing together as they got out of the car.

One boy, who looked ridiculously like Oliver, had been wearing football gear with soccer boots draped by their laces around his neck. Another had helped his mother carry shopping and the littlest one had tumbled on the front lawn for ages, playing with the family dog.

Such a nice, normal, happy family. *Except that she'd been making love with their father.* For four whole months! And all the time she'd known nothing of them, had believed Oliver loved only her. Had thought he was planning to marry her. What a silly, gullible little fool she'd been.

The experience had sent her scurrying back to the safe life of being a Goodman. Laura had drawn the Goodman shield around her like armour, because she knew without a doubt she wasn't cut out for anything but the security of love within a marriage.

Except that somehow Nick Farrell—who *suddenly* wasn't a stripper and wasn't married, but a widowed father and an upright citizen instead—made the thought of being an uptight, prim and proper Goodman less appealing.

It would be jolly nice if she could actually stop thinking about him completely, but ever since she'd met Nick she had been riding an emotional helter-skelter.

Even when she'd been appalled that he was
a stripper she'd loved the way he looked. His
amazing kiss had zapped her into a whole new
level of awareness and yet she'd been embarrassed ever since about her brazen response.

And then Nick had completely charmed her
with the skilful way he'd entertained the children at the hospital. And finally he'd intro-
duced her just now to those darling little moth-
erless girls…

And now…she couldn't pin down her feelings.

Of course she hadn't fallen in love with him
or anything ridiculous like that. It was something else she felt…a nervous excitement…a
puzzling need to think about him all the time.

During the photography session she was so
acutely aware of Nick's presence that she was
barely conscious of anyone else. She had trouble with her breathing whenever he came near.
On several occasions the photographer required them to link arms and she wondered if
Nick could hear her galloping heartbeats. His
touch electrified her.

Somehow she managed to mingle with the wedding guests and make the usual small talk. At some point they climbed into a limousine and drove to the reception. She presumed she ate the three-course-meal that was served to her. Vaguely, she listened to speeches and toasts.

All evening people told her she looked lovely, but the only time she really took any notice was when Nick paid her a polite compliment during his speech.

She might have lingered over his words if Susie hadn't leaned over and whispered to her, ''I'm so glad Nick made a straight speech. I was worried we might be in for some kind of practical joke. You know—pay-back for the hen-night.''

But Susie spoke too soon. Nick went on to read a pile of faxes and messages and his commentary was absolutely peppered with clever, teasing jokes. His comic timing was perfect and he left Rob red-faced and the guests breathless with laughter. Which is the real Nick? Laura wondered as she watched him.

The tender father, the brilliant Crown Prosecutor or the daredevil joker?

Long after he'd taken his seat once more, she sat there, lost in thought. What happened to all these roles when he turned into Nick the lover? His kiss had been sensational...

"Care to dance?"

The deep voice close behind her brought Laura out of her trance and back to the reception with a jolt. She realised that Susie and Rob had completed the bridal waltz and that other couples were now joining them on the dance floor.

Everyone would expect the best man and the bridesmaid to dance at least once. Feeling exceedingly self-conscious, she rose from her chair. She was intensely aware of Nick's hand at her back, gently guiding her past the other tables to the polished timber dance floor in the middle of the room.

She turned to face him, keeping her eyes lowered as she allowed him to take her right hand in his firm grasp while she placed her left hand on his broad shoulder. He tugged her a little closer and she heard the smile in his voice when he said, "I've been waiting to dance with you all evening."

Before she knew what was happening he hauled her against him and held her firmly and surely as he began to guide her around the floor.

She wondered if he could feel her trembling. Her skin tingled all over, she was so conscious of the strength of him and the underlying beauty of that body moving against hers.

Her mind threw up pictures of Susie's party. The way he'd playfully shown off his tanned, silky skin stretched over taut, manly muscles. Her stomach tightened as she thought of the dark trail of hair from his chest to his navel and beyond…all that maleness…all that hard muscle and strength so very close to her now.

His broad chest pressed against her and his thigh slid boldly between her legs as he pivoted her this way and that. And Laura's electrified body felt like a time bomb. A sleeping volcano, dormant no longer. She was remembering again what *lust* was all about.

When the music stopped, she thanked heaven that he didn't release his hold. There was every chance she would have melted bonelessly to the floor if he'd let her go. She felt his hand under her chin, lifting her face till her gaze was forced to meet with his, and her breath caught as she saw a familiar cheeky sparkle in his eyes. "Like to catch a breath of fresh air?" he asked. "I don't think anyone will notice if we're gone for a minute or two."

Oh, yes, please. Unable to speak, Laura nodded and allowed Nick to steer her through the tables that circled the dance floor. *How scary was this?* She was actually hoping that he was taking her outside to kiss her again.

She couldn't be changing this fast. What had happened to all that safe and cosy Goodman goodness?

Beyond the reception room, they passed through huge glass doors opening onto a balcony that overlooked the river. Nick guided her out of the lights and into the shadows and she was grateful for the breeze coming off the water to cool her heated skin.

She tried to distract herself from the urge to stare at him by leaning against the cool stone balustrade while she admired the lights from a nearby bridge.

"This is better," she heard him murmur close beside her in his rumbling, deep voice.

Too helpless to pretend uninterest, she turned his way. And he was looking at her with hot, hungry eyes. And suddenly she needed him to haul her into his arms and kiss her. *Now.*

She wasn't sure if it was because he read the urgent pleading in her eyes, but without saying another word Nick pulled her roughly to him and, just as she'd willed him to, he kissed her.

And...just as she'd known it would be, his kiss was perfect.

Not too tentative and not too brash, he took his time, letting his mouth roam over hers in confident, unrushed, seriously sexy caresses.

Laura knew she was being kissed by an expert. With lazy but insistent pressure, his warm mouth made love to hers slowly. He kissed her till she almost whimpered with pleasure. When his tongue teased her lips apart Laura had never felt so glad she was a woman.

She'd almost forgotten how wonderful it was to feel like this with a man.

But even in the past...she had never been kissed like *this*...by a man who knew *exactly* how to ask for what he wanted.

Nick didn't just invade her mouth. The taste and the heat of him invaded her senses. As he pressed against her, his body felt so hard and strong. So male.

She didn't care that she kissed Nick back with an enthusiasm that would leave him in no doubt about how she felt. She'd been Goody-goody Goodman for the past five years and tonight she suddenly wanted to be bad.

Gloriously, splendidly bad.

But finally Nick lifted his lips from hers and she felt his breath on her cheek as he whispered, "Pretty lady."

Breathless, she looked up at him. Had any man ever looked more divine? But, to her consternation, she noticed that he was frowning and looking pensive, as if he was suddenly upset about something. He took a step away from her, shoving his hands in his pockets.

Feeling a sudden chill, Laura wrapped her arms across her chest and hugged her arms, trying to ignore an awful sense of loneliness now she was out of his embrace. "Is something wrong?"

"Not wrong exactly," came his careful answer. "But I hadn't planned to kiss you like that."

"Oh," Laura replied in a tiny voice. "How did you plan to kiss me?"

"That's the point. I didn't plan on kissing you at all."

"I see." She counted a dozen thumping heartbeats while she let that news sink in. "Do you normally *plan* such things?"

"Oh, yes." He reinforced his words with a strong nod of his head. "Most definitely."

She lifted her chin. "That doesn't sound very romantic."

Nick had been staring straight in front of him, but now he edged his gaze warily towards Laura. "I don't suppose it does. But a man in my position can't afford to be too romantic."

She swung her shocked gaze back to the river. Nick Farrell *planned* kisses? It seemed such a sad idea to her. She planned the weekly roster for the library. She planned what she was going to cook for dinner and what she would write about in the next letter she sent her grandmother...but she never planned... romance.

Let's face it, she corrected her thoughts quickly, there had been nothing to plan. For at least five years now romance just hadn't been a factor in her life. "How do you go about planning your next kiss?" she asked, shooting him a sideways glance, but then she saw his slow grin and she felt very, very, foolish.

His lips quirked in a half-smile. "I find two volumes exceptionally useful—a telephone book and my diary."

What a fruitcake she was! A man in Nick's position, a man who was no longer married, but who found himself left with a mega-healthy, ultra-virile body, a demanding profession and an even more demanding home life...

Of course he would need to plan his...his social life. His *sex* life. She remembered with a guilty start that Oliver had been very precise about his liaisons with her.

"Of course," she said between gritted teeth. Then she tossed him a haughty glare. "So there's never any room in your life for spontaneity?"

He scratched his head thoughtfully. "What I'm trying to say, Laura, is that I don't want to give you the wrong idea. You're very lovely, and in the moonlight you look damn desirable—*heck,* it's not just the moonlight— you *are* incredibly desirable—but—"

He paused and Laura's heart seemed to shatter in her chest. She'd been buzzing with awareness of this man all evening. He'd just kissed her so comprehensively she could hardly remember her own name. He said she was desirable and she was feeling good about that.

Hallelujah! She was actually feeling good about a man's physical desire for her. After all this time since Oliver, that was a major break- through. She didn't want to hear any of his *buts.*

"*But* I don't think it would be very wise if we were to repeat a kiss like that."

Laura felt her shoulders stiffen. How dared Nick kiss her and then immediately dismiss it as a mistake. ''Why is it so unwise?'' she asked, and she was rather pleased with the cool and haughty edge in her voice.

Nick threw his dark head back to stare at the sky and spent several seconds studying the stars before he lowered his eyes again. Her heart thumped as she waited for his answer.

He looked at her almost gently. ''Pretty lady, I think if I were to kiss you for a third time I would also need to—'' He stopped again and Laura felt as if she was dangling from a very fragile string. ''Laura—I'm not looking for love.''

She gulped as she felt a ridiculous sense of panic surge in her chest. ''When did love come into this conversation?''

He frowned at her as if she'd missed something really obvious. ''I think, from the little I know of you, that you're the kind of woman who would need to love the man she went to bed with. And you would prefer him to love you in return.''

Laura swung away from him. She was completely shocked. She was furious. And she was mostly angry, because Nick Farrell, the clever lawyer, was three jumps ahead of her.

She felt as if she'd been left in the starting blocks while Nick was already halfway down the track. Staring at the black, silent river, she tried to keep her voice even as she asked, "How could you have the cheek to assume that just because I let you kiss me—that I would—that we would—?"

"You told me in the *way* you kissed me."

Laura glared at him. "It was just a *kiss!*"

Nick chuckled. "Laura, that old song got it wrong. A kiss isn't *just a kiss*. It has a language all of its own." He was grinning cheekily. "Am I right?"

"Oh, I'm sure you're always right."

"I thought we were telling each other something just now."

"Maybe you read me incorrectly," she replied. *Or maybe he'd read her dead right.*

Nick's face switched to serious mode again. "Please, forgive me if I'm wrong, but I figured your attitude to relationships might not be particularly—*relaxed.* I don't imagine you're into casual—''

Casual sex? She had been on the verge of thinking she could be tempted. *No she hadn't!* Laura closed her eyes so she wouldn't have to look at Nick. She didn't want to see how gorgeous he looked while she admitted to herself painfully that he had hit right on the truth. ''I am most definitely *not* into casual,'' she said coldly.

''You see, then, we're not a good match.''

Biting down hard on her lower lip, she held back an emotional retort. She could stay cool. She could do icy. She lifted her chin and stared back at him, her mouth pursed.

''Unfortunately,'' Nick went on less calmly, ''*I'm* not into deep and meaningful.''

''I can't imagine that's an ideal situation for your daughters—to see their father having a string of casual relationships.''

''That's my business,'' he snapped. ''But I can assure you that I'm aware of the problem. Discretion is vital, of course.''

Discretion, planning... Laura had never heard such a hard-headed approach to romance. She would have to make an addition to Nick's CV: Crown Prosecutor, father and...when it came to his love life, programmed robot.

He spoke again. "I've been in love once in my life."

She spun around, startled by his sudden admission and the depth of feeling in his voice. Her heart jerked painfully. "Your wife?" she whispered.

He nodded briefly. "Miranda."

Miranda. Laura repeated the name under her breath. Didn't that just sound like the name of the perfect woman? Beautiful, elegant to the core, a wonderful mother to those two little girls...

"Losing her was unbearable. I don't plan on ever loving someone that deeply again."

She saw the stark pain on Nick's face. His mouth had twisted into a cruel sneer. In his eyes she saw a ghastly emptiness that chilled her. He was reliving the pain of his wife's death and she couldn't bear to see the agony etched into his face. How badly he still hurt!

Something hard, like a steel band, clamped around Laura's chest. It was all so very clear now. Nick would never willingly expose his heart to that kind of pain again. And why should he when there were plenty of women who would be happy to accept his take-it-or-leave-it terms?

She was tempted to point out to Nick Farrell that he wasn't the only person who'd loved and lost. When she'd discovered how Oliver had deceived her she'd done her share of grieving. But she wouldn't mention that now.

"I'm sorry you've had to suffer like that," she told him. "And thank you for making your position clear." She flashed him a brilliant smile as she added, "I'm not quite sure where you stumbled on the notion that I wanted you to fall in love with me, but there's nothing like getting things out in the open right from the start. You can rest assured I have no ambitions in that direction. Now, if you don't mind, I need to go and attend to Susie. I'm sure I should be handing out wedding cake or helping her to get changed into her going-away outfit.''

Holding her head high, she swept past Nick without looking his way again.

CHAPTER FIVE

THE following Tuesday Nick's secretary was on a tea break when he arrived back at his office and found his phone ringing insistently.

"Farrell," he answered crisply as he tossed his wig onto his desk and his gown over the back of his chair. He was glad to have the day's gruelling session in court behind him.

"Oh, good afternoon, Mr Farrell," a feminine voice spoke. "I'm Diane Forrest, Felicity's teacher."

His hand, which had been working to loosen his collar and tie, stilled. "Yes?" he asked sharply. His heart thundered. *Dear God!* Had something happened to Fliss at school? *Please, no!* Four years ago he'd received a phone call just like this from a hospital—about Miranda.

He looked at his watch, but his eyes couldn't focus on the time. "How can I help you?" he asked as calmly as he could manage.

"I was hoping to be able to discuss one or two things with you about Felicity. I'm just a little concerned about her," the teacher continued.

A wave of relief flooded Nick. He closed his eyes for a moment and wondered how long it would take before he behaved calmly and rationally about his daughters' safety?

With effort, he dragged his thoughts from disaster to the likely concerns of a first-grade teacher. "I see. Is Fliss having learning problems?"

"No, nothing like that. She's a very bright little girl," came the reassuring reply. "But there has definitely been something bothering her lately."

The teacher made a small throat-clearing sound. "I hope you don't mind my saying this, Mr Farrell, but Felicity seems to be quite disturbed about your plans to marry again."

"What?" croaked Nick. "That's impossible!"

"It might seem impossible from your perspective, but there was an incident this morning that highlighted the fact that she's been quite distressed about the whole issue.''

"The reason I say it's impossible,'' Nick fired back, "is that I have absolutely no plans to marry again. I don't know how you got that idea, but I can assure you that such an event is simply not happening.''

"Oh?''

"There's never been any suggestion, any *mention* of a wed—'' Nick broke off as his mind flashed back to Saturday, to the memory of Fliss flinging her arms around him and announcing he should marry the pretty lady.

He groaned. "You said there was an incident this morning. What happened exactly?''

"The children were giving their morning talks,'' the teacher explained. "Felicity hasn't contributed for quite a while and so I thought it was time to encourage her to share some news. She stood out the front of the class and told us very proudly that her daddy was going to get married to a pretty lady. She seemed quite happy and excited about the news at first.''

"Did she?" Nick asked grimly. "So when did she become distressed?"

"Well, you know what little children are like. The rest of the class were allowed to ask questions and they bombarded Felicity for information about her new mother. Things like how old she is, what she looks like—if she can make chocolate cake. I could see she was getting upset and I called a halt to the questions, but I'm afraid the poor little kid broke down then. It took some time to calm her."

Still clutching the telephone receiver, Nick dropped into a chair, stunned by the teacher's account of his daughter's morning. Of course Fliss would have been upset when she realised what she'd done. She'd told a bald-faced lie to the class and they'd all accepted it as fact. She was intelligent enough to be overcome by guilt.

He wondered why on earth the silly muffin had done such a thing. This wedding business was obviously getting way out of hand. For days now the girls had been taking it in turns to traipse around the house with a mosquito net on their heads while carrying the bouquet

Laura had sent home. They were both wedding crazy.

"I had thought," the teacher continued carefully, "that there might be some unresolved issues regarding the new mother…maybe Felicity had some qualms about the changes ahead…but if you say you're not getting married then I guess we're dealing with a different issue."

Nick released a heavy sigh. "Indeed we are, Mrs Forrest. Thank you for letting me know about this, but I think I can deal with it at home. It's just that my daughter attended a wedding on the weekend and she has a vivid imagination. I don't think you'll have any more trouble with her."

"Oh, she's never any trouble."

"That's good to hear, but by all means let me know if you think she still seems unsettled."

"Certainly. I'm pleased there's not too much to concern us. Good afternoon, then, Mr Farrell."

"Afternoon and—thank you." Nick was about to drop the receiver back into its cradle, when he had second thoughts. "One moment."

"Yes?"

"This woman Felicity claimed I'm—er—marrying. Did she end up describing her?"

"Oh, yes." There was a slight chuckle on the other end of the line. "She was very definite. You were right when you said Felicity has a great imagination. She told us her new mother has lovely dark red hair and smiling blue eyes and she wears beautiful long, floaty gowns. Her classmates were very impressed."

"I see," said Nick, his voice grimmer than ever. "Thanks. That's all I need to know." This time he depressed the phone, dropped the receiver and flopped into his chair.

What the blazes was going on in his daughter's tiny mind? Leaning back, he blew out his breath as he linked his arms behind his head and stared at the ceiling.

He should never have allowed Heather to bring the girls to Rob's wedding.

"Little girls love weddings," she'd told him.

He'd finally consented because he valued his mother-in-law's opinion on the subject of what little girls liked and needed. And the girls were so fond of Rob. Let's face it, the guy had been like an uncle to them. But on the day of the wedding they'd hardly paid more than scant attention to Rob and Susie.

One look at that damn red-headed bridesmaid and they'd gone all dreamy-eyed. Then again, he acknowledged, one look at that same redhead and he'd become rather slow-witted himself.

How else could he explain the way he'd ended up out on the balcony with her, sharing that second incredible, molten kiss?

With another sigh he slumped deeper into his chair and slowly, without moving the rest of his body, stretched one hand forward and picked up a sheet of paper from his desk. It had some notes he no longer needed, so he crumpled it into a ball and tossed it towards the waste-paper basket in the corner.

It missed and rolled onto the carpet.

Nick swore. Wasn't that typical of the day he was having? He'd just finished a long session fighting one of the toughest courtroom battles he'd faced in his career so far. From the start he'd known without doubt that the accused was guilty, but it had taken every trick he'd ever learned to eventually nail him.

Now it looked as if, when he went home, he'd have an even tougher battle on his hands.

Today he'd eventually convinced the jury that the fellow in the dock was guilty of dealing in drugs. But he didn't like his chances of convincing his daughters to forget about Laura Goodman.

Laura sensed someone hovering at the desk near her, but she kept her eyes glued to her computer screen. On Wednesday evenings she always updated the catalogue files before she went home.

The person was leaning closer. ''Excuse me.''

Unable to avoid looking up, Laura discovered with a start that Nick Farrell's mother-in-law, Heather Cunningham, was trying to catch her attention. ''Oh, hello.''

"I'm so sorry to disturb you, Laura," the older woman said, "but I've brought the girls with me to borrow some books, and as I don't know much about the children's books that are available these days I wondered if I could get a little advice?"

Laura looked past Heather to see Kate and Felicity Farrell dressed in their school uniforms and standing in the children's book corner. They were staring in her direction.

Their shining eyes suggested they were brimming with suppressed excitement. Laura's heart slammed and thumped in her chest. She'd been trying so hard not to think about Nick, but seeing his girls brought a host of sensations—most of them uncomfortable.

Quickly saving the work she'd completed, she left the computer and joined Heather Cunningham at the desk. "Let's see what we can find."

"Just before we go over to the girls, Laura, I think I should warn you that they have been giving Nick rather a hard time because of you."

Laura's heart slammed and thumped some more. ''What have they been saying?''

Heather took a deep breath before replying. ''That bridesmaid's bouquet you sent home has meant endless games of weddings.'' She went on to explain that Felicity had made an embarrassing mistake at school.

Then she added, ''And yesterday afternoon Kate collected all her pocket money and her birthday money and demanded that I take her to my hairdresser and have her hair dyed red.''

''Good heavens!''

''Apparently Nick had to spend most of last night reassuring Kate that her light brown hair is beautiful.''

''Of course it is,'' Laura agreed weakly. Stunned by the woman's news, she looked across at Kate, who'd tired of waiting for them and found a book that interested her instead. Now she was sitting at a table to read it.

Her tawny hair fell in a fine silky curtain. ''When I was Kate's age I was teased dreadfully because of the colour of my hair. I would have given anything for nice, quietly coloured hair like that.''

Heather sighed. "Kate used to be happy that her hair was the same colour as her mother's. She is so much like Miranda."

Laura looked at Kate again, noting details. Slim and elfin-featured, the child had soft brown eyes and hair straight as a pin.

So that was what Miranda had looked like. That was the kind of quietly elegant woman Nick preferred. It couldn't be a more different look from her own fiery curls and hard-to-hide curves.

So what? Laura reminded herself sharply. What Nick Farrell thought of her appearance was irrelevant. He'd made that excruciatingly clear last weekend.

She frowned at Heather Cunningham. "If I'm causing trouble between the girls and Nick, why have you brought them here?"

The other woman looked uncomfortable for a moment. "The girls begged me to bring them, but actually I wanted to come anyhow, Laura. I wanted to warn you."

"Oh?" Laura replied, and she straightened her shoulders as she faced Heather Cunningham.

"You'd be foolish to develop any romantic notions about Nick."

Laura's eyes rounded with anger. "I don't indulge in romantic fantasies, Mrs Cunningham."

The other woman made a huffing noise. "You wouldn't be the first woman who's made a beeline for a widowed man, especially a handsome, well-to-do man."

Laura was so angry she refused to respond. A stretch of silence vibrated between the two women, then eventually she asked quietly, "What kind of books did you want the girls to borrow?"

Heather turned towards the Children's Corner. With a faint sniff, she said, "I don't think we should be encouraging these two to read fairy tales. I'd like to see them reading sensible books about animals or other parts of the world."

As she crossed the room Laura willed herself to ignore the spurt of affection she felt when Nick Farrell's bright eyed, sweet little daughters turned and smiled at her. Surely she could maintain the demeanour of a highly pro-

fessional, very efficient and impersonal librarian for the next ten minutes?

Felicity looked up at her and her grin widened. ''Hi, Laura. Can you please help me to
find a book that tells me about where babies
come from?''

Laura suppressed a groan of dismay. This
was going to be even harder than she feared.

Nick's secretary buzzed him late on Thursday
afternoon.

''There's a call coming through from someone who refuses to give his name, but he insists he must speak to you.''

''Put him on,'' Nick sighed. He was tired,
and for the past hour he'd been fantasising
about going home and catching an early night.

When he heard the line switch through, he
didn't care that his voice sounded weary as he
drawled, ''Nick Farrell speaking.''

''Is that Mr Farrell, the famous Crown
Prosecutor?''

Nick hesitated. For a minute he thought the
caller was Rob, playing another prank. But
Rob would hardly bother to call long distance

from his honeymoon on a tropical island. He'd have better things to do right now.

And besides, the voice was a shade too thick with irony to be a joke, the tone was too sinister.

He frowned as he replied. "As I said, it's Farrell here. Who's speaking, please?"

"Never mind who I am…what I have to say is more important."

Nick thought about hanging up, but there was a chance the caller was someone with a vital tip-off…someone wanting to alert the authorities but afraid and needing to stay anonymous.

"OK," he said carefully. "Talk to me. What information do you have?"

"I hope you're enjoying your hollow victory in the Stokes case, Mr Farrell."

"Stokes? What's this all about?" Nick's eyes narrowed. Warren Stokes was the fellow he'd had convicted of drug dealing. At a guess, this would be his brother, the thug who'd hurled abuse at him as he'd left the court. "Who are you? What do you want?"

"I just want to inform you that I'm about to get even with you, Farrell. You and your family. And it will be done in a most unpleasant and painful manner."

Anger and fear gripped Nick simultaneously. "Don't you dare threaten me and my—"

But before he could finish he heard the man's laugh and then the mocking burr of the dial tone, indicating his caller had already hung up.

The weekend at last! By one p.m. on Saturday Laura was grateful to be closing down the library and heading home for some peace and quiet.

Seven days since she'd seen Nick. With a little luck he would soon be a faint memory. A blip on her distant horizon.

Her post-Nick Farrell future might be looking dull, but it was definitely safe. Goodman-style safe.

Like most Saturday mornings, the library had been particularly busy, and she was nursing a faint but persistent headache.

Susie was still away and her replacement had to get home in time to transport her children to their afternoon sporting matches, so Laura had let her go early. Now she was closing windows, turning out lights and generally making sure everything was in order before she left.

As she gathered up her handbag and a thick novel to read that evening, she heard a muffled animal-like sound from behind a bookshelf nearby. Frowning, she tried to peer through the lower shelves. Without the lights on, it was hard to see, but she was sure there was a bulky shape on the floor.

She watched it for twenty seconds or so, and—*yes*—it moved. It not only moved, it grew. Someone had been crouching on the carpet and now he or she was standing.

''Who's there?'' she called, trying to sound calmer than she felt.

There was another muffled squeak and the sound of whispering.

''Come out of there!'' Laura ordered. If she had to face an intruder she would rather do so out in the open than in the shadowy aisles between bookshelves. Guerrilla tactics were not her forte.

As she watched, the shape became two shapes. Two small shapes. They moved past the rows of books. But even before they rounded the end of the shelf Laura guessed who was there. ''Kate and Felicity!''

Big eyes, one pair brown the other grey, looked timidly up at Laura.

''What are you doing here?'' she cried, and then added quickly, ''Are you alone?''

They nodded.

Laura scanned the library just to make sure. ''Why were you hiding?''

''We were waiting until you weren't busy any more,'' Kate offered.

Shaking her head in bewilderment, all Laura could think to do was to ask more questions. ''How did you get here?''

''We caught the bus,'' Felicity announced proudly.

''The *bus?*''

The little girl was bursting to tell of their adventure. ''It was easy. We walked to the bus stop at the end of our street and waited for the bus that said Glenwood on the front. And we both gave the man a dollar out of our money boxes and he told us when to get off.''

''Does—does your father know you're here?''

Suddenly Felicity's bravado evaporated. She looked sheepishly at her big sister.

''No,'' Kate answered softly. ''We didn't tell Daddy.''

''For heaven's sake, girls, he'll be worried sick. Where was he when you left home?''

''He was busy in the back garden fixing the sprinklers.''

''What about your grandmother—Mrs Cunningham? Does she know anything about this?'' Slowly, they shook their heads.

Laura's mouth dropped open. It looked very much as if these girls had run away from their father—to *her*. She pressed a palm against her throbbing forehead. ''So why have you come here?'' she asked weakly.

They looked at each other as if for help. It was a question they seemed to have difficulty answering.

"Did you want to borrow more books?"
She would have been very surprised if they'd
already read the pile they'd borrowed the other
day.

"No thank you," Kate answered politely.

Felicity chewed her lower lip and looked
worried. "We just wanted to see you again,"
she said in a small voice.

Laura looked down into the little girl's big
grey eyes, so like her father's, and her easily
softened heart melted as quickly as an ice
cream on a tropical beach.

She dropped to the floor and crouched beside Felicity, taking the girl's small hand in her
own. "Sweetheart," she said warmly, "it's
lovely to see you." Glancing towards Kate,
she added, "but your daddy will be terribly
worried about you, won't he?"

Kate nodded.

"Actually," Laura said, jumping quickly to
her feet again, "I should ring him straight
away and tell him you're safe."

The girls followed her as she walked back
to the main desk. "What's your number?"

As Laura dialled the digits Kate gave her she felt her breathing constrict. The last thing she wanted to do was to ring Nick Farrell with this kind of news. How could she start? She prayed for inspiration as she heard the ringing on the other end of the line, and her heartbeats picked up pace.

But there was no answer. She left a brief message on his answering machine.

"Your poor father is probably scouring the city searching for you," she told them as she put the phone down again. "You know you should get straight home."

They nodded.

"How about I walk you to the bus stop and you can catch a bus home?"

"We don't have any more money," admitted Kate.

Laura frowned at the child. She was only seven years old, but really! "Kate, if you're big enough to bring your little sister on an adventure like this, you should know better than to leave home with only enough money for a one-way ticket."

On cue, two fat tears spilled from Kate's big brown eyes.

Oh, Christmas! Laura thought. What am I thinking? I don't have any choice. I can't just throw these two onto a bus. I'll have to take them back to Nick's place.

The thought of facing the lion in his den made her head throb more fiercely than ever. "Don't worry," she quickly reassured Kate, in spite of her desire to stay as far away from Nick as possible. "I'll drive you home."

The girl breathed a huge sigh of relief and, almost immediately, her face broke into a grin. "Thank you."

"Goody!" squeaked Felicity, and the little imp almost skipped with delight.

Laura did her best to ignore the stirring suspicion that these young misses were plotting something. Suppressing a resigned sigh, she swung her bag over one shoulder and took the girls' hands.

During the trip across three suburbs Nick's daughters kept up an incessant patter—mostly information about their father. Information

Laura hadn't asked for. Details she didn't want to know. Of course she didn't.

"You don't have to tell me all your father's secrets," she tried to protest.

But they ignored her.

"Daddy's favourite meal is coral trout with Thai salad," Kate told her.

"He likes to listen to boring grown-up music," added Felicity. "Sympathy orchestras."

"And he always drinks his coffee black."

When she tried to distract them by asking questions about the books they'd borrowed from the library they answered briefly then hurried on to tell her that Nick swam forty laps of their pool every day to keep his body nice and muscly.

"He cooks really yummy nachos."

"And he makes great strawberry milkshakes using real strawberries."

Their encyclopaedic account of their father's habits kept flowing and, against her will, Laura kept seeing images of Nick.

She could picture him late at night in a darkened room, listening to classical music. *She loved classical music.*

She could see him in his kitchen, laughing with his daughters as he fed them nachos dripping with melted cheese. *She loved Mexican food.*

She could picture him early in the morning, diving into a pool, looking divine in his bathers. *She loved...*

"Tell me more about yourselves," she suggested.

"Every Christmas Daddy takes us to visit Grandma and Grandpa Farrell," Kate told her.

"They live way up north on a farm," Felicity added. "They've got lots of friends."

"And does Daddy have lots of friends?" Laura asked, and then immediately wished she'd bitten her tongue. She really didn't want to know the answer to that.

The girls must have sensed the loaded nature of the question. They didn't answer straight away, and Laura was concentrating on driving so she didn't see their faces, but she knew there was a short period of silent communication between them.

"Don't worry. I shouldn't have asked that," she said quickly.

"No," responded Kate just as quickly. "It's OK. Actually," she added in a solemn little voice, "Daddy doesn't have many friends."

"He's very lonely," piped in Felicity.

"'Cos we're all he's got," Kate explained. "And we're only little."

"He needs the companionship of a good woman," Kate added finally, with the air of a politician announcing the solution to the nation's economic crisis.

"Good grief!" cried Laura, so shocked she almost missed a turn. "Where on earth did that idea come from."

"Everyone says so," intoned the little girl darkly.

Everyone except the man in question, thought Laura. "You girls wouldn't be trying your hand at matchmaking, would you?"

Two pairs of eyes rounded with practised innocence. "What's matchmaking?" Kate asked.

"Never mind," sighed Laura. But the thought that the girls were like their father— three jumps ahead of her—left her feeling jit-

tery and confused as she pulled up outside the
address they had given.

She took a deep breath and cursed her headache, which was worse than ever now. Peering
through the windscreen, she inspected Nick
Farrell's house. She might have guessed it
would be impressive. The contemporary timber and glass construction was set back in a
beautiful natural bush garden.

"It doesn't look as if Daddy is home," Kate
announced.

Laura followed her gaze to the open garage
door and saw the empty parking bay. "I guess
we'll just have to wait for him," she said with
a sigh.

"Come and wait for him inside," Kate
urged.

"You have a key?"

Kate reached beneath the neck of her T-shirt
and with a triumphant cry of *"Ta-da,"* pro-
duced a key on a silver chain. "Come inside
and I'll make you a cold drink." She sounded
very grown up, but spoiled it when her face
broke into an impish grin.

A cold drink was just what Laura needed. She could down a couple of aspirin at the same time. Without further question, she followed the girls as they led her through a slate-paved entrance into a large, beautiful living room with polished hardwood floors and pristine white walls.

At the far end of the room, floor to ceiling windows looked out into a lush green rainforest. It was a surprisingly peaceful room—spacious and airy and decorated in a minimalist style with only a few pieces of casual, but expensive-looking furniture. The high-raked ceilings were lined with honey-coloured timber and, through the far windows, a soft green light filtered through the trees.

There was no traffic noise. All she could hear were the faint sounds of birds calling to one another in the canopy outside.

Tasteful, relaxing…extremely expensive.

"You can sit here if you like," Kate said, pointing to a cane lounger lined with plump cushions covered in a navy and white batik print.

She sank gratefully onto the lounger and, with excited giggles, Kate and Felicity left the room. Laura let her head fall back against the cushions and realised that her neck and shoulders were horribly tense.

No doubt the tension had been the cause of her headache. Tension in her shoulders—tension made worse by the fact that she still had to face a certain angry thirty-something daddy she was trying desperately to avoid.

But surely no self-respecting headache would hang around in a room as restful as this.

The girls were back again very quickly. Kate carried a tray with three tumblers of bright red cordial. Felicity followed with a jug holding more of the same gaudily coloured liquid.

Painkillers and red cordial? It sounded a touch dicey, Laura thought as she reached for her handbag and sorted through the jumble of tissues, make-up, hairpins and keys till she found a packet of aspirin. As she straightened again she felt a clunk as her head hit the tray Kate held and she heard the girl's horrified cry.

Seconds later cold liquid was running through her hair, soaking into her shirt front and trickling down the back of her neck.

"Sorry!"

Laura jumped to her feet as tumblers bounced onto the timber floor around her. Thank heavens they were plastic. Kate stared at her in dismay while Felicity stood, looking worried and clutching the jug tightly to her chest as if she was afraid it would suddenly spill as well.

"Oh, dear. Your shirt!" Kate cried.

Laura looked at her front. This *couldn't* be happening. Her white linen shirt was soaked pink and red. The fabric clung to her chest in sticky wet patches. Her head throbbed. Kate wailed dramatically.

"It'll wash out," Laura muttered. "Can I get a cloth from the kitchen to mop it up?"

"You should have a shower."

"No. It's OK. I'll just dry it for now."

"But do you want Daddy to see you looking like that?" the child asked, and she stared pointedly at Laura's chest.

Laura looked down at her shirt-front again, eyeing the way her lacy bra and—*cringe*—her nipples showed through the damp fabric. ''I guess it is a bit revealing.''

''And your hair's all sticky,'' commented Felicity.

When Laura thought about bearding the lion in his den with sticky hair and a decidedly transparent shirt, she had to agree that it wasn't the most helpful armour for a battle.

''The bathroom is this way,'' Kate was saying, and she'd already covered half the distance to the hallway door as if the matter of a shower had already been decided.

Laura snapped two tablets from the foil pack in her hand and swallowed them with a gulp of cordial from Felicity's jug. Ur-rgh! The mixture was way too strong. No wonder she was sticky. She followed Kate down a hallway and to a door at the end of the passage.

It opened into a spacious bathroom. Nick's bathroom. Terracotta floor, white-tiled walls, nifty black fittings. An old shirt—one he might use in the garden—hung on a hook behind the door.

In a wicker hamper she could see a jumble of masculine clothes waiting to be washed. A pair of jocks dotted with the ace of spades lay on the floor beside it as if they'd been tossed towards the hamper and missed.

Nick Farrell's underwear.

Laura dragged her eyes elsewhere.

A black and silver can of deodorant stood on the bench next to the hand basin and there was a razor with little bits of shaving cream still clinging to it next to a cut-glass bottle of expensive-looking aftershave.

A fluffy white towel, still damp from his wet body, hung on a rail nearby.

Laura could almost sense Nick here in the room. Naked. Steamy. The hair on his chest still damp and his body sleek and shiny.

Oh, help, she thought, and all her good work in the past week telling herself that she didn't care a fig about Nick Farrell was undone in an instant.

"Um." She gulped, realising that Kate was still watching her. She reached towards a stack of towels piled neatly on a shiny metal rack. "Can I take one of these clean towels?"

"Sure." Kate nodded. "And the shower's through there."

"Thanks."

The little girl left and Laura dropped her clothes into a heap on the floor and crossed the room to the glassed-in shower recess. She let the warm water wash over her and tried to shake off the headache and the weird feeling that she was losing her grip.

Her life seemed to be slipping sideways in a direction way out of her control, and for a control freak it was a nerve-wracking notion.

She thought again about the way that cordial had spilt. Had she imagined it, or had Kate been leaning over her as she straightened? A seven-year-old couldn't have planned that *accident*, could she?

Surely not.

Her suspicions were getting out of hand.

Why would Kate plan to land Laura in her father's bathroom, soaping herself with the same bar of soap that had slithered over his sexy body not so long ago?

Give it a miss! she groaned as she reached for a bottle of shampoo and lathered her hair.

Concentrate on how you're going to explain your way out of this mess. She stuck her head under the stream of water to rinse her hair and wondered how Nick was feeling right now.

No doubt he was scouring the suburbs, searching for his daughters. Was he frantic with worry? Would he be relieved or angry when he found them?

As she turned off the taps she heard a ferocious roar coming from somewhere within the house. Her stomach clenched as she realised her questions would soon be answered.

The lion had returned to his den!

And this was supposed to be an ordinary Saturday. What had she done to deserve being thrust into a nightmare? Her heart thudded as she dashed out of the shower to snatch up the towel.

Nervously, she quickly dried herself. But she was only halfway through the process when the bathroom door flew open and a tall, wild-looking figure rushed in.

Clutching the towel in front of her, she saw sheer panic in Nick's eyes. His face was sheet-white and his thick dark hair was dishevelled as if he'd run his hands through it many times. "Where are they?" he shouted.

The sound of running footsteps in the hall sent him swinging back in that direction.

"Daddy!"

When he saw the girls he slumped against the wall with relief, his breath escaping in noisy grunts. The whole sequence only took a matter of seconds, but it was enough. Those few short seconds showed Laura the astonishing depth of Nick's emotion—an insight into the love—*and fear*—this man had for his daughters.

Despite the fact that she stood naked and dripping, in *his* bathroom, her heart twisted painfully and tears sprang to her eyes.

But Nick seemed to recover quickly from his initial reaction. He gave the girls swift hard hugs before turning back to glare at Laura. "You've got a hell of a lot of explaining to do."

CHAPTER SIX

NICK'S fists clenched as he willed his breathing and heart rate to slow. OK, the girls appeared to be unharmed. Thank God! But he couldn't believe that this pesky redhead was back in his life.

Not just in his life—in his *damn bathroom!* He blinked. She was wrapped in nothing but a towel.

''What have you been doing with my daughters?''

''This isn't how it looks,'' Laura cried, her face set in an angry scowl as if she were ready for battle. ''I didn't just invade your house and your shower.''

''Oh, no?'' he asked coldly. He didn't believe one word.

First she'd worn feathers, now a towel. What was it with this woman? She seemed to spend half her life draped in next to nothing

127

and then the rest of the time trying to make excuses for it.

Except today she was also damp and pink from a recent shower. Her hair clung to her head and neck and its colour was amazing when it was wet. Shining damply against her pale skin, it looked richer, darker, more luxurious and intriguing than ever. And her limbs extending from beyond the towel were distractingly shapely.

But what the hell was she doing in his bathroom?

"If you give me a moment to get dressed, I'll explain everything," Laura said.

"Tell me now."

"Daddy," he heard Kate cry, "don't blame Laura."

He patted his daughter's head. "You girls go and wait in your room. I just have to sort something out with Miss Goodman."

"But, Daddy," Felicity chimed in, "don't be mad at her."

Of course he was mad at her. He'd been through hell this morning. How could he *not* be mad at her? With Thursday's menacing phone call ringing in his ears, he'd spent three hours in torment, trying to trace his girls.

"Girls," he ordered coldly, "I told you to go and wait for me in your room."

"But she doesn't have anything to wear," Kate squeaked.

"I don't? Where are my clothes?" This came from Laura.

"I've put them in the washing machine."

Nick frowned. He didn't like that guilty flash in Kate's eyes. What was going on here?

"We spilt red cordial on her," explained Felicity.

"Accidentally," Kate added quickly.

"*Cordial?*" He ran desperate fingers through his hair. This was getting crazier by the minute. He looked from Laura to his daughters and back to the librarian again. "You'd better have a good excuse for this."

She glared at him fiercely and clutched the towel around her as if she feared it might be ripped away at any minute. But she sounded surprisingly cool as she said from between gritted teeth, "Is that how a Crown Prosecutor works? You yell accusations first and ask questions later?''

He dropped his voice a dozen decibels. ''I'm not yelling.''

''You most certainly were yelling, and before you accuse me of a crime, Mr Farrell, perhaps you should listen to the evidence.''

He narrowed his eyes. ''The evidence? You've turned up uninvited in my home—'' He was forced to pause. He'd been about to make reference to her nakedness and her bold use of his bathroom but, for the sake of the girls, he deleted those comments. ''I find you here with my daughters after they've been missing for *three* hours. I'd say that's plenty of evidence.''

Laura's plump bottom lip stuck out as she blew a strand of damp hair out of her eyes and Nick did his best to ignore how sexy the action looked.

''Kate,'' she said softly, ''you should do what your father has asked and take Felicity to your room. I'll explain to him what happened.''

To Nick's annoyance Kate, who hadn't budged when he'd given his orders, looked at Laura with big trusting eyes and then grabbed her sister's hand and dragged her back down the hallway.

What had happened to family loyalty?

He snapped his angry gaze back to the red-head in the towel. "This explanation had better be good and it had better be fast."

"I can't believe you're this upset just because you think the girls have been with *me*." Her smooth shoulders rose and fell as she drew a deep breath. "I'm not a convicted criminal, Nick. I'm not even a stranger. In case you've forgotten, just a week ago I was a bridesmaid at your best friend's wedding. Your girls were perfectly safe with me," she informed him icily and, before he could comment, she kept talking. "They caught a bus to the library. I couldn't let them come back on their own, so of course I had to drive them. And then there was the little incident with the cordial."

"They went to the library? Why?"

"I don't really know why they came. They said they wanted to see me."

Nick groaned. He thought he'd convinced Kate and Felicity to get over their obsession with Laura Goodman. For the past two nights there had been no mention of her—or of weddings. He'd been sure that silly phase was over.

"But don't take my word for it," she said, interrupting his thoughts. "You have two star witnesses waiting in their bedroom. Why don't you ask them?"

"Yes," he said with a rueful grimace. Of course, his daughters were quite capable of telling him what had happened. "I will check out the girls' story." He shot her another narrow-eyed glance. "You'd better get dry while I speak to them."

A wet curl flopped back into her eyes and she tossed her head sideways, trying to flick it away without letting go of the towel.

Nick shoved his hand into his pocket in case he gave in to the temptation to help her.

Looking around her and nodding towards a shirt hanging on the back of the door, Laura asked, "Can I wear that for now?"

"Sure." He shrugged as casually as he could and stepped back as she shut the door firmly in his face.

It took Nick two minutes to check out Laura's story with the girls. He returned, grim-faced, down the hall to the bathroom and she opened the door at the same moment he arrived.

Now the towel was looped tightly around her hips like a sarong and Nick's shirt hung loosely over the top, but not so loosely that he wasn't acutely aware of her naked breasts beneath the fine white cotton.

Damn!

"Fetching outfit," he said, hoping he sounded cool and unmoved.

"It's not meant to impress you," she snapped.

Ouch! That put him in his place. He cracked a smile as he began to walk on down the hall.

"Nick!" she called from behind him.

Slowly, he turned back her way.

"What did the girls say?"

"Your stories matched," he admitted reluctantly.

"Then I'd like an apology!"

"Oh."

"*Oh?* Is that all you can say?" Her blue eyes blazed. "Don't you think I deserve one? I know you're supposed to be a whiz-bang prosecutor, but we've told you I'm not guilty."

"You're right, I should apologise," he said softly, and he stepped towards her. Then, incredibly, of its own accord, his hand reached out and Nick found himself tucking the cutest little curling wisp of damp hair behind Laura's ear.

Her ear was exquisitely dainty. In the very centre of its lobe nestled a tiny pearl. His hand stayed there, because he suddenly needed to know everything about that delicate, soft little piece of her.

"What—what are you doing?"

He looked at her, startled. How could he answer? He didn't have a clue what he was doing. "I'm apologising," he said, dry-mouthed.

"I accept your apology," she whispered.

"That's settled, then." He pulled his hand away abruptly and was distinctly unhappy with himself.

Laura was looking unhappy, too.

He shouldn't have touched her. Why on earth had he done that? He was in the middle of setting the woman straight.

Laura cleared her throat. "I'd like to make something clear," she said. "Perhaps you were so ready to blame me because you're worried that I'm chasing after you?"

Still feeling bewildered, he shook his head.

"You don't have to worry that I didn't understand your lecture last week," she continued in an excessively chilly tone. "I'm not trying to worm my way into your life. I know perfectly well that you made a hideous mistake when you kissed me."

Nick grunted. Had it really been a mistake to kiss Laura? It was becoming difficult to remember why. The fact that she was wearing hardly any clothes was clouding his thinking. His anger might have cooled, but in other ways he was definitely growing hot and steamy.

"I'm not after you," Laura insisted. "I'm not interested in you. If I had my way, I would never see you again."

Nick knew a response was expected, but right now all he could manage was to shrug and to continue down the hall.

From behind him, Laura called, ''If you really want to know, I don't give a—a rat's *bum* about you!''

It dawned on Nick, then, that perhaps the lady was protesting too much.

And *that* was a sobering thought.

It forced him to remember what was really going on here. Neither of them could afford to give in to fleeting feelings of attraction. She wasn't a woman he could fool around with and he couldn't match up to the committed man of her dreams.

That was the bottom line.

That was why she'd looked so shocked and angry when he'd touched her.

As he reached the kitchen he asked over his shoulder, ''How about I make us some coffee while you're waiting for your clothes to dry?''

She stormed into the room after him. ''Forget coffee. I'd choke on it.''

''If you don't mind, I'll make one for myself.''

"Suit yourself."

The phone rang.

And in an instant Nick's lustful thoughts died and his heart rate doubled. Laura was closest to the phone and her hand jerked towards it in an automatic response.

"Leave it!" Nick snatched the receiver. "Nick Farrell."

"Mr Farrell," replied a male voice. A slimy voice that brought the hairs standing up on the back of Nick's neck. "So nice to speak again. You remember me, of course?"

It was the voice he'd come to detest.

"I know what you're up to, Stokes," Nick snarled, "and it won't work with me. Go threaten someone else or come out in the open and face me."

"Let's not be melodramatic," the voice simpered. "I just wanted to let you know what a delightful time I've been having this afternoon watching your mother-in-law, Mrs Cunningham. Would you like to know what she's doing right at this minute?"

Nick's stomach lurched. "You're spying on Heather? For God's sake, why?" He caught Laura's wide and worried eyes watching him.

"She looks after little Kate and Felicity every afternoon after school, doesn't she?"

The girls! Nick swore loudly. This was the first time the caller had mentioned his daughters. His legs turned to sawdust and he sagged against the kitchen bench.

"Right now Mrs Cunningham's snipping the dead heads off roses in her front garden. She keeps a nice garden, doesn't she? I'll enjoy taking a closer look at it when I come next week for your daughters."

"This isn't going to help your brother," Nick shouted. But before he could continue he heard the click of the receiver being replaced.

With an angry cry, he dropped his phone back into its cradle. His heart pounded. Sick and shaking, he slumped onto a kitchen stool and let his head drop into his hands.

He groaned as he fought off nightmarish images of Kate's and Felicity's terrified faces as a dark, mad stranger approached them.

"Nick?"

He lifted his hands away from his face. Laura was leaning towards him, her eyes brimming with concern.

"It was a nuisance call," he told her. "There have been others. The family of a crim I prosecuted last week took exception to one of their relatives going to jail."

"What does he want?"

"He's making threats about stalking the girls and Heather."

"That's terrible," she whispered, white-faced. After a thoughtful pause, she asked, "What are you going to do?"

"I'll get back to the police." He sighed again, feeling suddenly exhausted. "But, bad as it sounds to us, as far as the police are concerned we only have a low-level threat at this stage."

"But if this man's spying on the girls?"

Nick swallowed back a wave of nausea. "What I'd really like to do is take time off and get the hell out of here with them."

Laura seemed to think about that for a minute or two. "But could you just hide indefinitely?"

"No," he admitted with a sigh. "What I need is a safe house. It looks like this guy knows the girls' daily routine. He knows they go to Heather's. I need to find somewhere he wouldn't know about. I'd send them up to my parents' place on the Atherton Tableland, except my dad's going into hospital for some tests. Mum has more than enough on her plate, what with worrying about him and the fact that it's almost harvest time."

Laura nodded in silent agreement. "Rob and Susie get back from their honeymoon tomorrow," she said slowly. "They're setting up house at Susie's place."

Nick rolled his eyes. "That would be great, wouldn't it? Rob could carry Susie, Kate *and* Fliss over the threshold of his nuptial home."

Laura's mouth quirked. "I'm sure they wouldn't refuse to help you out, but OK— maybe it's not the best option."

She switched her gaze to a spot on the wall, and she stood there deep in thought.

"I don't expect you to worry about this," he said.

"No wonder you were out of your mind when the girls disappeared this morning."

"Yeah. This guy has certainly put the wind up me. That's just what he wants, of course. It's probably all bluff, but I can't risk it." He grimaced and ran tense fingers through his hair.

Still staring at the wall, Laura nodded. Then she turned back to him. "He'd be unlikely to know anything about me, would he?"

"No...you should be safe." There was something about her expression, a kind of dawning determination in her bright blue eyes, that made Nick frown. "What are you thinking?"

He realised she was looking very earnest now—like the Laura he'd first met—the *do-gooder*. The woman who'd somehow conned him into doing a clown stint at a children's hospital. "It's not *your* safety you're thinking about, is it?" he asked.

"No," she said softly.

"Oh, no," he said. "Don't even begin to think about trying to help us."

Laura smiled faintly. "What's the use of being a born-in-the-womb do-gooder if I don't put all those helpful impulses into practice when they're really needed?"

Nick swallowed. "Are you thinking what I think you're thinking?"

"I'm thinking the girls would be safe at my place. Nobody knows we're—connected."

"But, Laura—"

"Tomorrow's Sunday and I have Monday off. That's at least two days the girls can be in a safe house with twenty-four-hour supervision while the police track this fellow down."

He stared at her, surprised at how calm and collected she sounded. "But you don't have kids. Do you know anything about looking after little girls? They can be quite a handful."

She folded her arms across her chest. "I happen to have excellent qualifications."

"Really?" Nick was aware he sounded as if he was in court as he asked, "Would you care to elaborate?"

Laura lifted her chin and eyed him haughtily. "Apart from the library work I do with children every week, I have even more useful credentials—I've spent several years of my life *being* a little girl.''

His mouth twitched into an unwilling smile, but then he frowned again. He hardly knew this woman. Half an hour ago he'd been ready to evict her from his home and his life. ''I couldn't impose on you like that,'' he began, but even to his ears his objection didn't sound strong enough.

Maybe that was because, deep down, he suspected that Laura would probably be a rather satisfactory solution to this dilemma.

''It's no skin off my nose either way. You can take it or leave it, Nick, but I wouldn't offer if I wasn't happy to help out.''

Nick looked at her and forced himself to ignore the towel draped around her hips. He noted instead the open honesty and genuine compassion revealed in her expressive face.

''This is a terrible situation for Kate and Felicity,'' Laura continued. ''My house isn't very big, but I have a spare bedroom with two beds in it. I live in a quiet street and my neighbours are very respectable.'' Her eyes flashed him a blue challenge. "And I like your girls. I think we could get on just fine."

Nick made a frantic mental list of his alternatives. His lawyer friends? Their wives were either career driven or ladies-who-lunched. They wouldn't have time for his daughters. There were a few stray bachelor mates, but they would run a mile before taking on such a task.

As for his female acquaintances, Nick grimaced at the thought of asking any of them to become involved in his domestic affairs. They might misinterpret his intentions and see it as a step towards the altar.

He had a sneaking suspicion that Laura Goodman was his only safe option.

Laura was standing with her arms crossed, waiting for him to comment. "I realise you'd prefer for the girls to be with someone you know better. Why don't you just think of me as a last resort?"

Maybe he was panicking and not thinking clearly, but Nick found himself saying, "I have to admit that Kate and Felicity trust you, Laura. They wouldn't be frightened to go with you.'' He raised an arm and rubbed the back of his neck thoughtfully. ''But we'd need to think up a convincing reason.''

Actually, Nick suspected there was every chance the girls would stampede to be with Laura whether he unearthed a good reason or not. Again, he ran a restless hand through his hair. ''But there's another problem.''

''Oh?''

''Kate and Fliss have some silly ideas about us. This past week, they've...''

''Been trying their hand at matchmaking?''

His head jerked up, startled. ''Yeah. How did you know?''

''They've been working on me, too. They've made sure I know your favourite food, your taste in music, how hard you work at keeping in shape.''

Nick released a low whistle. ''The little devils.''

''I understand that you are very lonely and need the love of a good woman.''

''They said that?''

''They did.'' She grinned. ''But I didn't believe it.''

Nick managed an answering grin and found himself asking, ''And you also didn't believe I have to work hard to keep in shape, do you?''

That question seemed to catch her out. She didn't answer at first and then she said, ''Look, Nick, I'd only take the girls to my place if we had a very clear understanding that I'm not in any way trying to win your affection.''

''Sure.''

''We probably can't stop the girls from having their little fantasies, but at least *we* know how things are.''

''I guess so,'' he agreed. ''We can both work at snapping them out of these silly ideas.'' He shook his head. ''I never should have let them go to Rob and Susie's wedding.''

''If you decide to let the girls come with me, I'll do my best to make sure they understand I'm simply a friend and that's all.''

He let out a deep breath. ''Thanks. That— that would be helpful. I'd really appreciate it.''

''I can't see that our relationship or lack of one needs to be an issue.''

Nick nodded. "You're right. It shouldn't be an issue."

However, he thought guiltily, what he didn't add was that it wouldn't be an issue once Laura was dressed properly again. It wouldn't be an issue just as soon as he stopped fantasising about her throwing off that towel and moving, naked and lovely, up close against him.

"Of course you'll want to keep in close contact. You could visit us in the evenings."

"Uh—evenings?"

"The girls will want to see you."

"Yes, of course." He struggled to clean up his mind.

Reaching over to the pen and notepaper beside the phone, Laura wrote down her contact details. "It would probably be best if you don't drive straight up to the front door—just in case anyone's watching. Heaven forbid. There's a lane at the back of my house. Come around that way. Use the back door."

She handed him the address.

"Right," Nick murmured, feeling dazed as he stood staring at Laura's neat handwriting outlining her addresses and phone numbers for home and work. "Thanks. That's terrific."

But what wasn't terrific, he realised, was that spending his evenings at Laura Goodman's house sounded far too much like the recurring dream that had been bothering him all week.

CHAPTER SEVEN

ON MONDAY morning, Nick looked up from his paperwork to find Rob, coffee-cup in hand, standing in the doorway of his office.

"Ah!" he exclaimed with a smile. "The worn out, glowing image of a man just back from his short but sweet honeymoon. How are you, mate?"

Rob's answering grin broadened. "I'm not feeling too bad at all. I have to admit married life doesn't seem to have done me any harm."

He settled himself into a chair opposite Nick. "But you must be feeling pretty good yourself. What's this Susie tells me about your kids moving in with Laura Goodman? That sounds very cosy. And darn quick work."

"It's not how it looks," Nick muttered, the smile dropping from his face.

"Pull the other one," laughed Rob. "Laura's a stunner. But I must admit it's not like you to be so predictable, Nick."

149

"What on earth's predictable about it?"

"The best man getting it on with the brides-maid."

Nick shot Rob a withering glance. "Use your brains, Rob. You're talking about Laura Goodman. I don't know how well you know her, but think Girl Guides, Florence Nightingale—Pollyanna. The woman's simply doing me a good turn."

"Whatever you want to call it," Rob replied with a chuckle.

Nick shook his head in exasperation. "You're barking up the wrong tree."

But he could understand Rob's scepticism. Any man who didn't know Laura—who responded purely to the way she looked—would think she was one hot babe. Those fiery curls, her flashing blue eyes and come-to-me curves were so very deceptive.

It was hard to believe that underneath all that she was innocent and earnest.

Or was she?

All weekend he'd found himself thinking about Laura and it had been like deciphering a difficult but intriguing puzzle. Take the way

Laura spent most of her time acting like Little Miss Never-Been-Kissed, and yet when he'd kissed her she'd known exactly what to do with her mouth.

Those sorts of thoughts had been tormenting him more and more frequently. He'd begun to imagine how things might have been if he hadn't backed off from that second kiss. If he hadn't made such a mess of trying to explain about Miranda.

Maybe he'd jumped the gun when he assumed Laura wouldn't be interested in a casual encounter…

Rob's voice cut through his thoughts. ''You're not trying to tell me that Prince Charming has been turned down?''

''It's a waste of time even thinking about her that way.''

His mate's smile was sly. ''But you are thinking of her that way, aren't you?''

''Not worth it.'' Nick paid careful attention to his desk calendar.

''Yeah, well, in your case it's probably not worth wasting time on a non-starter. Plenty more fish in the ocean just waiting to be caught by Nick Farrell.''

Rob leaned back in his chair and favoured his friend with a knowing grin. ''Problem is, you're just not used to a woman who plays hard to get. You've had far too many women throwing themselves at you. But believe me, mate, the ones who start out saying no are worth the struggle.'' He chuckled fondly. ''My Susie took an advanced degree in brush-offs.''

''Don't bore me with the details.''

But Rob wasn't giving up. ''The secret is to just lay things out in the open and see what happens.''

Nick made a point of looking at his watch and frowning.

''Treat her with respect, but put the hard word on her. You'd be surprised how many modern chicks just want you to go with your caveman instincts. And that's a fact.''

Letting out his breath on a long sigh, Nick decided it was time to put an end to Rob's endless flow of useless advice. ''Try listening to these facts, Rob.''

He leaned closer and lowered his voice. "There's a whacko sending me threatening phone calls—the Stokes case; I think it's the brother—threatening the girls. *That's* why Kate and Felicity are at Laura's."

In a flash Rob's grin and all mention of seduction, with or without finesse, vanished. Nick knew he could trust Rob to take him seriously on this.

"The girls are OK about going to Laura's?" Rob asked.

"I've spun them a story that I'm getting ready for a big case and need to do a lot of extra preparation at night and their grandmother is too busy with charity work to take them this week. They don't mind. They think Laura's the cat's pyjamas."

Rob nodded and, to Nick's relief, the two friends spent the next fifteen minutes discussing the stalker and the strategies Nick and the police had in place. They didn't mention Laura again.

As she closed the door on the girls' bedroom, Laura's telephone rang. She hurried through to the kitchen.

Nick spoke. "I've been held up at a meeting. Are the girls still awake?"

"I've just settled them," she told him, and she heard his stifled sigh. "I'm sorry you missed them, but they dropped off to sleep much more quickly this evening than last night. Tonight I only had to tell them one story. Last night it took three."

"They were very excited when I left them last night, weren't they?"

"Yes, and they were disappointed they missed you tonight."

"I'm really sorry." After a pause, he asked, "So what kind of a day did you three have?"

"Oh, we spent the morning baking and decorating gingerbread shapes, and this afternoon we made clothes for their teddy bears. I found some patterns in a magazine."

There was a lengthy silence on the other end of the line.

"Nick?"

"I was just thinking what a great time they must be having—doing all that girl stuff. They don't get much of that with me."

"It's hardly surprising, Nick, and I'm sure they don't mind. The only complaint I heard was that you don't keep a box with scraps of fabric."

"Well, no, I don't."

"But they tell me you're teaching them to cook."

"Just very simple things," he agreed. "When Miranda died I had to go out and take cooking lessons. I couldn't do much more than boil water. I don't want them getting caught out like that."

Laura's fingers twisted the phone cord. She saw a sudden picture of Nick, at home alone with his daughters, dealing with his grief and struggling to learn how to cook. The thought caused a curious prickle in her throat.

After an awkward silence, she asked, "So you haven't had any more threatening phone calls?"

There was a loud sigh. "No. The sneaky devil seems to be lying low. He's probably guessed the police are taping my calls."

"Maybe he's given up?"

"I wouldn't bank on it. Not yet at any rate. That's another thing I wanted to tell you. The girls should go to school tomorrow. I know you're due back at work, and Kate and Fliss will wonder what's up if we keep them at home any longer. I've alerted their teachers. They'll be extra watchful."

"That's fine. I can drop them at school in the morning and I don't mind keeping them with me at night for a little longer."

"Thanks, Laura. I really appreciate everything you're doing." His naturally beautiful voice sounded unexpectedly genuine. It was almost as if something deep and meaningful passed down the phone line.

Laura decided she must have been mistaken. Nick didn't do deep and meaningful. Not with her at any rate, but of course his feelings for the girls were another matter. She tried to put herself in his shoes and to imagine the strong bond he must feel with his little daughters.

"Are you calling from work?" she asked.

"Yeah. I'm just about to leave. Why?"

''I thought you might like to call by. You could take a quick peek at the girls even though they're asleep.''

''Thanks, I'd like that.'' Nick's reply was enthusiastic. ''I'll be there in ten.''

As Laura replaced the phone she wondered if she'd been a little too impulsive, inviting Nick to call by. The thought of him arriving at her house without the girls around to distract him made her feel suddenly nervous.

But she decided that was a silly reaction. She'd made it patently clear on several occasions that she wasn't setting her cap at him. In her bathroom, she tidied her hair and freshened her lipstick. ''I've got this situation and this man under control,'' she told her reflection.

Her reflection didn't look as convinced as she would have liked.

Fifteen minutes later, Nick stepped into the girls' low-ceilinged bedroom. There was just enough lamplight for him to see his daughters lying sound asleep in two little timber beds with soft white coverlets. A familiar, warm glow curled around his heart as he looked at them.

He was amazed that after just two days he missed these little rascals so much.

Fliss lay with her dark curls spread in a glossy tangle against the snowy pillow. Cuddled tightly in her chubby arms was Sir Joseph, her worn and tattered but much loved bear.

In the other bed was Kate in her favourite sleeping position, sprawled on her back with her mouth slightly open. Her neat pink bear, Princess Tina, sat proudly on top of the little cupboard next to her.

Nick guessed that the smart white and gold satin gown the bear wore was a legacy of the day's activities.

He looked around him. The blue-carpeted room held little more than a glossy white cupboard and the beds. Everything about it was simple, fresh and clean. Between the beds was a small circular window.

It was set deeply into the white stone wall and a gauzy curtain trimmed with thin stripes of blue satin ribbon fluttered in a breeze drifting in from the garden. Through the round window he could see the silhouette of a pine tree and the evening star shining brightly. For some reason, coming to Laura's house made Nick feel as if he was stepping into a fairy tale. No wonder the girls were happy here. It would be like living in a storybook. ''Looks like the girls have made themselves at home,'' he whispered.

Laura's eyes shone as she nodded and then quietly led him outside. She closed the door again and he followed her down a passage, past a closed door, which he guessed would be her bedroom, to her sitting room.

She indicated with a slightly awkward flutter of one hand that he should take a seat, so he lowered himself just a little uneasily into a chair upholstered in a dainty floral.

''Have you eaten?'' she began.

''Yes, thanks. I'm fine. We had a snack at the meeting.''

''Would you like some tea or coffee?''

''Coffee would be great. Thanks.''

She hurried away quickly before he could add another comment. Not that he knew what else to say, now. This was the second time he'd been to Laura's house but he still felt strangely self-conscious. Out of place.

He looked round him at the artistic clutter of honey-toned antiques, hand-hooked rugs and stained glass lamps. On a circular table, at his elbow, there was a collection of blue and white porcelain, and over near the window thriving plants spilled out of glowing copper pots.

Every wall was lined with bookshelves and crammed full of books. Her story book cottage was so folksy and cute it could have been photographed for one of those country-cottage magazines.

He found the house intriguing and puzzling...inexplicably attractive...adult and innocent...like Laura.   Everything here was so different from the contemporary minimalist decor of his house, it made him feel like an outsider.

Was it her feminine touch that made the difference? He felt a jab of uncertainty. Were his girls missing out on something intangible but vitally important that he could never give them?

He was still lost in thought when Laura walked quietly back into the room carrying a wicker tray, which she set down on the coffee table. As she poured fragrant-smelling coffee into two mugs and handed him one, he asked politely, ''Have the girls been behaving themselves for you?''

''They've been very good,'' she said with a warm smile that made a little dimple in her cheek, not far from her mouth.

Nick's eyes rested on her soft pink mouth.

''Honestly, they're no trouble at all. I'm enjoying having them here.'' She looked up from her task and the deep beautiful blue of her eyes almost took his breath away.

She shook her head and smiled. ''But you might have warned me. I didn't know I was going to have to make up so many bedtime stories.''

He sipped the coffee. ''So they demanded a story about a princess?''

''How did you guess?''

''Kate always wants stories about princesses.''

''Does she always get them?''

He chuckled. ''As long as she's prepared to have my style of princess. One who's lost in space or climbing a snow-capped mountain.''

Laura smiled. ''Tonight we had a princess who lives in a castle and loves pink.''

''That would have made a very pleasant change. What happens?''

''You don't really want to hear a children's story.''

''Why not? I might learn something. I need to get a better handle on how small females think.''

''Well...'' She hesitated for a moment, but then seemed to gather courage as she told him, ''This princess insists that everything in her castle must be pink. Pink carpets, pink curtains, pink walls, you name it.''

''Food?''

''Oh, yes, of course,'' she said with a laugh. ''She lives on pink jelly, pink ham and pink lemonade.''

''Sounds great,'' he said, and he meant it. After the stories he told, where the princesses always ended battling their way through jungles or risking their necks deep-sea diving, the girls would have loved Laura's feminine slant.

Hey, he loved it. He could just picture Laura in pink—in a pink bedroom with pink satin bed sheets. *Enough of that.* "So what happens next?"

Laura sipped at her coffee and her eyes widened. "You don't really want the whole plot, do you?"

"Sure."

She relaxed back in her chair, rested her elbow on its arm and propped her chin in her hand. Nick watched the dainty chin resting on her hand and wanted his hand there. Wanted to be touching her. Her skin looked impossibly soft.

"Well...the princess gets tired of pink and wants everything changed to blue," she explained.

He smiled. "That's typical of every princess I know."

Laura looked at him sharply, as if she was wondering exactly *which* princesses he referred to. But she didn't question him, just went on with her story. "I'm summarising, of course, but after a while she gets tired of blue. Having everything blue can become depressing.''

''Indeed. So after she gets over the blues, she tries yellow? That's a happy colour.''

''It is, isn't it? The girls and I decided if you could catch a laugh and put it in a jar it would be yellow.''

''Did you?'' Nick was suddenly spellbound by the thought of Laura and his girls capturing happiness in a jar. True happiness was such an elusive slippery emotion.

He could picture Laura laughing as she told her story in the cosy little blue and white bedroom. He could imagine her stopping patiently from time to time to let the excited girls join in and he felt something like a small skyscraper blocking his throat.

''Anyhow, you've got the gist of the plot,'' Laura went on. ''The princess finally gives yellow the flick and then green.'' By now she was smiling broadly, but then her smile faded and he watched as she twisted the handle of her mug between two slim fingers. The gesture looked nervous, as if she was reminding herself that she mustn't relax. Mustn't let down her guard.

"So, come on," he coaxed, trying to distract her. "You can't leave me dangling. You've got to tell me how the story ends."

She rolled her eyes at him. "What happens in every good story when a princess finds herself in a mess?"

Her question caught him flat footed. Nick stared at her. "A princess in a mess?" he repeated slowly. No. He wouldn't think about the stalker or his daughters. The girls were safe here. "She hires a lawyer?" he said, and tried for a grin.

Laura shook her head. "Not this princess."

"Then obviously she relies on magic. Or failing that she uses her brains and gets herself out of the mess."

Laura let out a groan. "Blast. I didn't think of that, but now I wish I had."

"Don't tell me she's rescued by some twerp of a prince and they get married and live happily ever after?"

She looked away, pursing her mouth into a tight little pout. "It was the Rainbow Prince, actually. Kate's idea and quite appropriate, I thought.''

Nick couldn't resist teasing her. ''Surely you could have thought of something more— *now*. These girls are growing up in Australia in the twenty-first century after all.''

Unexpectedly, her blue eyes blazed angrily. ''You mean I should have left the princess happily or perhaps even miserably *single?* Avoid a married and happily ever after ending at all costs?''

''Why not?'' he asked with a defensive shrug. ''I don't believe in happily ever after. It's an impossible promise.''

Laura looked stricken. ''But they're only children, Nick. They have to dream.''

Nick was very much aware that this conversation had taken a definite turn for the worse. Stepping into quicksand would be safer than discussing marriage with Laura Goodman. ''Dreaming needs a touch of reality or it becomes dangerous.''

Her eyes flashed with another spurt of annoyance. ''I'm sure your daughters get enough realistic endings in *your* stories. I thought I did jolly well coming up with any kind of story at all. I'm a reader and a librarian, not a writer, not a story*teller*.''

''You *did* do well,'' Nick said, suddenly contrite. ''I apologise. And I'm inordinately grateful to you for taking the girls under your wing. It really is very generous of you.'' He sent her his warmest smile. ''And, in case you haven't noticed, they think you're ace. Better than Christmas.''

''I'm happy to have them here.'' Primly, she replaced her mug on the coffee table and folded her arms across her chest. Then she looked at him as if to say, We've had coffee, so why are you hanging around?

For some unfathomable reason, Nick felt the skin on his neck burn.

Laura didn't say anything more. She just sat there, watching him, as if she was waiting for him either to leave or start discussing international politics or the decline of the Australian dollar. He noticed that she'd begun to chew her lower lip. Why was she suddenly nervous?

Heck. He was nervous. What *was* he doing here? He'd checked on the girls. He'd finished his coffee. It was time to go. He sat forward. He should start walking. Straight out of this cottage. Right now. The muscles in his legs tensed as he prepared to stand.

But once he was on his feet Nick found that he hated the idea of leaving. He began to walk towards Laura instead of away, and next minute he was reaching down to her and taking her hands in his. When she didn't resist, he pulled her out of her chair till she stood close in front of him.

And then he knew exactly why he had stayed.

CHAPTER EIGHT

LAURA couldn't believe that Nick was standing so close and looking at her *that* way. That way of his...the way that made her feel incredibly female but far too melting and helpless.

His eyes were so dark and hot it was impossible to ignore their signals.

And it was dreadfully hard to ignore her own wild desire. Part of her, a very insistent part of her, wanted him to pull her close and kiss her again...and again...

But she knew it was madness and she'd made all those promises about keeping her distance. Somehow, she found the courage to hold him at bay. "Don't tell me you've written me into your diary?" she asked shakily. "Is that why you came here tonight?"

Nick frowned. "I thought you invited me."

Laura gave an exasperated shake of her head. "But last week you explained about your need for planning your social life and here you are—alone with me on a quiet Monday night and you knew the girls were already sound asleep.''

''I didn't plan *this* at all. I've never yet planned to kiss you, Laura.''

''I see,'' she whispered.

With gentle fingers, he touched her cheek. ''But you keep taking me by surprise. You're so stunningly sexy.''

''Sexy?'' she croaked, genuinely shocked. If Nick had told her she was pretty, she might have believed him. But *sexy?* Nick *who-brought-a-room-full-of-women-to-their-knees* Farrell? How could that man think she, Laura Goodman, was sexy?

''You're incredibly sexy,'' he murmured, his eyes checking her out in a slow-burning appraisal. His thumb stroked her cheek. ''You have such an angelic face and yet you have all this sinfully fiery hair.''

His hand drew a line down her neck to her breast and she shivered. ''And you have this beautiful, sensuous body. You're a deadly combination, Laura. You pretend to be so strait-laced but it's all a disguise, isn't it?''

''Of course not,'' she snapped.

But her response was automatic, springing out of five years of habit. When she looked up at Nick, she wasn't so sure any more. ''I—I don't know,'' she amended.

''I think we should find out.''

In sheer self-defense, Laura closed her eyes. She couldn't keep looking at Nick. When he looked at her *that* way, the man was instant temptation. No need to add water. Her will power was on the edge of total disintegration. Any minute now, he would pull her just a little closer. He would kiss her again.

And she knew that she wanted him to. She would give in. Oh, yes, she would give in to the sensational experience of Nick's mouth taking hers, of his strong arms wrapping her close.

And, yes, he was right. Whenever he was around she felt wildly sexy. He made her want to forget she was a Goodman. He made her want to forget everything except that with him she should take a few risks. Surely it would be worth it?

He leaned his face towards hers and she felt the masculine roughness of his chin against her soft cheek. One breath later and his mouth was moving over hers, tasting, and demanding. Seducing…

"You—really—are—" Nick murmured slowly between kisses as he trailed his lips over her face, "very—very—sexy." His hands slid beneath the loose hem of her shirt and she felt melting and wanton as his touch lingered over her skin. "You feel unbelievably soft. Lovely…"

Oh, help! I'm lost, Laura thought. But then something in her head screamed, *hold it!*

And, just in time, she remembered.

She remembered that this was Nick, The Man Who Loved Miranda. Only Miranda. The man who had explained in careful detail just exactly why they shouldn't be doing this.

With a little cry, she sprang away from him.

"What is it?"

Her mouth trembled slightly. "How could you have forgotten that I'm not interested in flings? You told me last week that you could tell at a glance I'm not into casual sex. And you explained very clearly that you're not interested in anything else. So what on earth were you thinking when you started kissing me again?''

''I—'' Nick shrugged.

''How could you forget we're so different?'' Laura persisted. ''You shouldn't be putting all this pressure on me! You were going out of your way to seduce me!''

Nick smiled slowly. ''And you liked it.''

Oh, yes. She *had* liked it. She'd *loved* it. But she didn't need this ego on legs to tell her so. ''That's beside the point.''

''No, Laura,'' he said quietly, confidently. ''It *is* the point. We've been driving each other crazy with this on-again off-again caper. The best thing we can do for each other is to stop all these silly inhibitions and respond to our basic needs.''

''Basic needs?'' Here he was again, talking about romance as if it were nothing more than a biological process. ''How pleasant you make it sound.''

"I'm sure it will be."

"*Will be?*" she cried. "Are you crazy?"

"I don't think so. I'm considered sane by most people I know."

"This isn't a time to be smart," she snapped. "You can't expect me to just say—Yes, Nick, that sounds like a great idea. The bedroom's the first door on the right."

He had the bald-faced temerity to grin. "Why not?"

She couldn't hold back the sudden tears that stung her eyes and burned her throat. "You really want to make love to me just like that? Like I'm an item in your diary?" Her voice cracked, but she forced herself to continue. "After all that noble talk you gave me at Susie's wedding, about how sensitive you are to my—to my values—you expect me to agree to a tacky affair with no emotion, no romance and no commitment?"

He looked back at her and his eyes, his beautiful grey eyes, looked suddenly empty. Bewildered.

Laura bit back on a sob. It was a fleeting impression, but for a minute Nick had looked like a little boy who'd lost his way.

Stepping away from her, he crossed her sitting room and stood in the doorway. His grey eyes still had that empty look—like the sky when there's no chance of sunshine. "It simply occurred to me that it really is time for some action on my part," he drawled. "But I won't take up any more of your time."

Laura's mouth drooped open. "So you're going?"

"Of course."

"Just like that? You mean that if I was prepared to—to fall in with your plans, you would have been happy to spend half the night here, but as I'm not you're rushing off because you're wasting your time?"

He stood looking grim but didn't answer.

Laura made an angry, shooing gesture with her hands. "You'd better go, Nick. Whatever you do, don't waste your precious time. I'm sure I can't afford your hourly rate."

"Look, calm down," he grumbled. "It was simply a suggestion from one adult to another, not a submission for a bill to be passed by parliament.'' He let out his breath on a sudden sigh. ''But let's not start a fight now when we have much more serious things to concentrate on.''

Laura grabbed the back of a chair for support. She could feel panic rising in her like liquid. She was drowning in it. Despite her protests, her mind had been running out of control—like a movie projector, flashing up images of Nick and her. Together. Making love. Hot. Happy. Loving. Love.

''Of course,'' she managed to say as, with a supreme effort, she pushed those pictures aside. ''I'm more than willing to concentrate on serious things. As I said earlier, I'm quite happy to take the girls to school in the morning. And I can take a few minutes off in the afternoon to pick them up. They can stay at the library with me till closing time.''

''It's a lot to ask.''

''I've said I don't mind, Nick.'' Her voice sounded cracked and full of tears, but too bad. He couldn't mess her around like this and expect her to be unmoved.

"It should only be for another day or two. This rat-bag caller will probably show his hand again soon and then we should be able to nail him." He stepped forward as if he might touch her—or kiss her on the cheek. She tilted her cheek in his direction—just a little.

But he didn't kiss her. Instead, he frowned and stepped back again sharply, and shoved his hands deep in his trouser pockets. "I'll let myself out the back way. Goodnight, Laura."

"Goodnight."

She didn't watch him go. She stayed where she was in her little lamp-lit sitting room at the front of the house. And she listened to the sounds of Nick leaving. His footsteps retreated down the hall and through the kitchen.

She heard him unlock the door. There was the slight squeak of the hinge as he let himself out and the solid click of the door closing again. And she listened to his progress back down the path at the side of the house and out of the front drive and she felt tears swell in fat pools and begin to slide down her cheeks.

For a minute or two there was silence outside, but she continued to stand there listening and crying silently. And then, from some distance away, she heard a car door slamming and an engine starting up. There was the spurt of acceleration. And finally the sound of Nick driving away.

A noisy sob escaped Laura as she slumped into an armchair. What on earth was the matter with her? She should be proud of herself. She'd resisted the temptation to give in to something she didn't believe in. Nick had suggested a casual romp. A fling. Turning him down was right.

Two days ago, she and Nick had agreed that their relationship should remain strictly within the bounds of friendship. Then his testosterone had spoiled everything. Thank heavens she'd said no and saved herself from inevitable heartache. She was on the moral high ground. There was absolutely nothing for her to feel bad about.

So why did she feel so unhappy?

Why was misery soaking through her like grey, drizzling rain?

*   *   *

"My, what a long face!" Susie rushed up to Laura. "Nothing's happened to the girls, has it?"

"No, no, they're fine." Laura sighed and pushed a stray curl out of her eyes, and frowned at her computer screen as she scrolled through the catalogue. She had several jobs she wanted to clear before the library doors opened this morning.

Beside her, Susie folded her arms across her chest and leaned back against the counter. Her eyes narrowed and Laura could sense that her friend was studying her intently.

"And how is their daddy?" she asked slowly.

"What's that?" Laura squinted at the computer screen, paying studious attention to the location details of an obscure book she was trying to track down.

"You heard me, Laura. I asked, how's Nick?"

"How would I know?"

Susie sighed, and muttered, "I imagine you've had some kind of communication with him in the past twenty-four hours."

Laura pulled an uninterested face. "He just called to check that the girls were OK."

Susie moved to the after-hours return box and hefted out an armful of books, plonked them on the counter, and then turned back to Laura. "You and Nick must have become pals pretty quickly. You met a fortnight ago and already you're minding his kids."

Suppressing an angry sigh, Laura took some notes about the book before closing down the screen. The last thing she needed this morning was an in-depth discussion of her relationship with Nick Farrell.

She looked up at Susie. "You know what I'm like. I'm always a sucker for the grand gesture. As soon as I heard Nick's problem I offered to help out. It seemed logical that as hardly anyone knows I'm in any way connected to Nick, the girls should be safe with me."

"Mmm," mused Susie. "But the tiny detail you've avoided sharing with me, my dear best friend, is the precise nature of this connection you have with Nick that hardly anyone knows about."

"The *precise* nature?"

"Yes."

"Well, to be precise, it's a platonic connection," Laura snapped. "And, Susie, I expect that should answer all your *friendly* questions in one go."

"It doesn't answer my first question," Susie said softly.

"What was that?"

"Why you're wearing such a long face. You've insisted that Nick's girls are fine, and he's fine, but I've never seen you looking so miserable."

Laura looked away. It was useless to protest that she was fine, too. She knew Susie wouldn't believe her. "It's too hard to explain," she said.

"Try me."

"Oh, Susie, you wouldn't understand. You don't have any hang-ups about the opposite sex."

"Laura, we all get hung up about the guys we really care about."

Laura stiffened.

"How many times have you seen Nick since the wedding?"

"A few times. Nothing—like a date. Nothing serious."

Susie smiled knowingly. "You don't have to go on a date for there to be sparks flying." Casually, she began to fiddle with the books she'd stacked in front of her, opening them to expose their bar codes. "And that's what we're talking about, isn't it? Sparks? At a guess I'd say serious sparkage."

"I'm not sure."

Susie rolled her eyes. "She's not sure," she said to the ceiling. "Laura, I saw you guys at the wedding reception. There was enough electricity on that dance floor to short circuit the wiring of the entire hotel. And that was before you went outside."

Laura's teeth clenched. "Are you going to check those books in, or are you just going to play with them all day?"

"I'll check them in," Susie replied. "Keep your hair on. But listen, honey, Rob tells me that Nick Farrell is a really great guy. I'm talking True Blue. Not just a good-looking stud, but a really nice fellow.''

''I'm sure he's a monument to male perfection,'' Laura replied icily. ''And I understand his wife was perfect, too. The perfect couple.''

''His wife?'' Susie frowned. ''Is that what this is all about? But she's in the past, Laura.''

''Try telling Nick that.''

''Oh.''

''Nick's heart and soul still belong to Miranda. He's not going to trust them with anyone else. All he wants from a woman is a casual fling. No emotional contact, something purely physical.''

''Oh,'' Susie said again.

''Now where's all your good advice?'' Laura cried, flinging the words at her friend.

Susie worried her upper lip with her teeth. ''I take it you haven't put him to the test?''

''I beg your pardon?''

''I mean, he's made all these claims before you two actually...'' She hesitated and frowned at Laura. ''Have you two—?''

''I told you it's platonic. Of course we haven't.''

"So—I reckon you could change his mind."

Laura couldn't hold back a bitter laugh. "Dream on," she scoffed, shaking her head. There were certain things even a best friend could never understand. Especially not a best friend who had just come back from her honeymoon. "Just leave it, Suze. Nick and I have agreed that we're incompatible."

Laura was happy with how definite she'd made that sound, but, as she stood there, scowling at Susie, she remembered the question she'd thrown at Nick last night. *You expect me to agree to a tacky affair with no emotion, no romance and no commitment?* And she remembered that fleeting sadness she'd seen in his eyes.

"Laura, if persuading Nick that you're incompatible makes you look this sad, I think you should reconsider."

Laura let out another weary sigh. There was no doubt she had just spent a night of utter misery. She'd lain alone and thought about Nick till close on dawn. "You really think I should agree to a casual affair?"

"Darling, when a man and a woman first meet they have to start somewhere. It usually takes time to move from casual affairs to cosy commitment."

"Of course I know that. But Nick's different. He told me right from the start that he's not prepared to love or commit to anyone else. And as for me, after Oliver I'm much more cautious about how I hand out my—er—affection."

"Give me a break, Laura, you've had five years of caution since Oliver."

Wasn't that the truth? Laura thought grimly. And being cautious hadn't exactly brought a barrel of laughs—or a sense of contentment.

"And as for Nick, I still think you could change his mind," Susie continued confidently. "He's only a man after all. And we all know men are dead scared about serious relationships and commitment." She smiled a beaming grin. "*Until* they meet the right woman."

Laura shook her head but Susie wasn't to be put off. "That's why I say you should put him to the test. Go with your natural urges and then watch him try to walk away from you. My guess is he could find it a darn sight harder than he thinks.''

With a disbelieving roll of her eyes, Laura turned back to her desk. But, in spite of her outward rejection of Susie's suggestion she found it intriguing. Should she really take a risk and just grab a handful of happiness with Nick?

He'd certainly managed to rattle her safe old sense of contentment. After two heart-stopping kisses—two-and-a-half kisses, if she counted last night—she was beginning to think that when a man like Nick paid a woman attention even a Goody-two-shoes should think about her short-term happiness before all else.

If she was honest, she was getting rather tired of her independence. Lately it had felt more like loneliness. As she riffled through an assortment of hanging files the thought lingered, teasing her.

Should she really give Susie's advice a try?

Heather Cunningham was in the library around mid-morning. She was the last in the line to check out books and she approached the desk with a serious, wary expression.

Laura pinned on a bright smile and thanked her lucky stars that Susie was in a back room, sorting new stock. "Hello, Mrs Cunningham."

"Good morning, Laura. How are my little granddaughters?"

Despite the awkwardness of their previous meeting, Laura was determined to be pleasant to Nick's mother-in-law. She filled her in about the girls' activities and finished by adding, "You must telephone them and have a chat one evening. I'm sure they're missing you."

Heather Cunningham's eyebrows rose as if she hadn't expected such an offer. "Thank you, Laura. I shall do that."

"I hope you haven't had any trouble from the stalker."

"No, thank heavens," Heather replied, and then her face softened a fraction. "You know, I'm actually rather pleased that Nick trusts you with Kate and Felicity."

Laura hid her surprise by stacking Heather's books neatly on the counter and inserting a bookmark stamped with the due date.

''The fact that he trusts you is a good sign,'' Heather continued.

''It is?''

''He can't go on trying to do everything for the girls for ever.'' Heather leant forward to confide. ''I know I was warning you off Nick last week, Laura, but if the dear boy's chosen you to help him out in this terrible situation I accept his judgement. Normally he never lets any of his women-friends near the girls.''

''Well, there's a subtle but vital difference between me and Nick's other women friends,'' Laura explained darkly. ''I'm not a—girl-friend. I'm just a friend who has a spare room and happens to be female.''

Heather nodded and her face broke into a surprisingly conspiratorial smile. ''Yes, my dear, Nick went to an extraordinary amount of trouble to explain that to me, too. In fact I was quite comforted by the way he went to such enormous lengths to make your situation crystal-clear.''

Puzzled by the knowing twinkle in Heather's eyes, Laura frowned. "Of course, no woman could replace Miranda," she suggested and she tried to ignore the spiteful voice in her head that whispered, *Saint Miranda, Miranda the Mother Superior.*

"Perhaps," Heather sighed. "But it's time Nick got over that."

Laura sensed her jaw dropping so quickly she half expected to feel it hit the floor. After all, this woman was Miranda's mother. She took a deep breath and said nervously, "Nick can't let her go, can he?"

"He's certainly finding it very difficult." Heather looked around the library. It wasn't very busy that morning. There was no one nearby. "Laura, it might help if I explain something."

Laura nodded uncertainly as she felt an embarrassingly desperate urge to hear whatever Heather could tell her about Nick.

"Nick needs very firm handling from any woman who loves him."

"But I don't—"

"My daughter set her cap at young Nick very early," Heather hurried to explain. "She decided she was going to marry him when she was sixteen. After that, she virtually never let him out of her sight. She worked very hard at being the perfect companion. Miranda even forced herself to study law—just so she could be with him at university. And, believe me, she had no natural inclination for the subject."

"That's—that's dedication."

"She was very keen to get Nick married and in the family way," the other woman said grimly.

Laura frowned.

"Kate was born just six months after the wedding." Heather's eyes shimmered as she looked at Laura. "Don't get me wrong, pet. I loved my daughter, but she was always insecure and that made her manipulative. The problem was," Miranda's mother went on, "after they were married and the girls came along, and Miranda was busy with them, Nick's career began to take off. They couldn't be together as often. Nick was working long hours and doing extra court work. He would

often have to travel to trials in regional cen-
tres.''

''Miranda was jealous?''

''I'm afraid so. She started going out in the
evenings to make Nick jealous. Going to night
clubs, of all places. I don't think she ever went
out with another man. She was just making a
statement. And then—'' Heather sighed deeply
''—one rainy evening there was an accident.''

''How terrible,'' Laura murmured. She was
shocked by this picture of Miranda—so different from the picture of sainthood she'd imagined. It sounded as if Nick's wife had been
very high maintenance. ''Did Nick feel guilty
that he'd made Miranda unhappy?'' she asked.

''Yes. The silly boy thinks the crash would
never have happened if he'd paid her more attention. But I know he did his best. We all did.
But Miranda needed too much.''

''I must say I'm surprised that you're telling
me this.''

Heather's eyes studied Laura for a moment.
''I've watched Nick mourning my daughter for
four long years. I love that boy, Laura. He's

not just the father of my granddaughters. He's the son I never had.''

''But none of this has anything to do with me.''

''Don't be too sure of that, Laura.''

''What do you mean?''

''You're a smart girl. I'll leave you to think about it.''

As Heather walked away, Laura suddenly felt she had far too much to think about.

Nick was having a bad afternoon. He couldn't concentrate on the case he was preparing. To start with, every time the phone rang he reacted badly. Stokes, the nuisance caller, had been silent for too long and that made him suspicious…edgy. Just what was the guy up to?

But there were other things adding to his edginess. Like the way he'd stuffed up last night with Laura. He was supposed to be an intelligent, clear-thinking, hotshot lawyer, but in dealing with Laura he'd sure fused a few wires in the old brain circuitry.

So much for Rob's bright advice. *Just put the hard word on her.* What an idiot he'd been to try that! He'd known instinctively that kind of approach wouldn't work and yet he'd gone ahead and tried it anyhow.

And now, the million-dollar question was *why?* Why had he persisted in making moves on this woman when he knew she was an unlikely candidate?

The questions without answers had rolled around in his brain, driving him out of the office to seek out a coffee in his favourite Victory Street café. He wanted to clear his mind of red hair and blue eyes and pale, pale skin.

But the problem was he couldn't just ignore Laura when she was doing such a magnificent job of helping him out. He really admired her for that. It was brave and generous of her to go out of her way for a couple of little girls she hardly knew. Next time he saw her he would have to try to make amends.

He would have to apologise.

Again.

Staring mulishly at his cup of espresso, Nick wondered if it would be better to try the *actions speak louder than words* approach. But that was a challenge in itself. It called for some kind of sincere gesture. Roses and chocolates were too *ho-hum*. Obviously, he couldn't take her out to dinner. She was otherwise committed with his daughters.

But—he smiled as a new idea revealed itself—he could cook for her. He could cook her dinner at her place. Nick played with that idea for a minute or two. Yeah. That was the way to go about making amends. She was putting herself out to take care of his girls. Dinner was a practical way to help out. And to show off what a sensitive New Age guy he really was. Not that he was trying to impress her, of course. Just thank her.

He sauntered over to the café's magazine rack, picked up this month's copy of the popular *Dine-In* magazine and flicked through its pages, deciding he'd cook her something new and trendy.

He liked the sound of the Low-Stress-High-Impress section. Steamed coral trout in soy and oyster sauce…wild mushroom risotto…they both sounded rather good.

Feeling better at the thought of positive action, Nick bought the magazine and, as he marched briskly back to work, he could almost smile at the thought of surprising the librarian with something as safe as food.

His secretary looked up as he walked through the door. "Ms Goodman is on the line. Shall I put the call through to your desk?"

Something in the region of Nick's chest did a double take. "Thanks." He nodded and hurried into his private office. Swinging the door closed behind him, he snatched up the phone quickly. "Nick here."

"Hello, Nick. This is Laura." Her voice sounded tight, worried.

"What's happened? Where are the girls?"

"They're OK. They're here. There's nothing the matter."

His sigh of relief was unavoidably noisy. He really had to stop carrying on like this. "Sorry I jumped on you. Slight case of overreaction."

"I—I just wanted to keep you up to date. I'm calling from the library. The girls have finished school. I was able to pick them up without any problems and they're here with me now. Kate's actually doing her homework and Felicity's in the toy corner. They've had some crackers and milk and they're both fine.''

''That's really good news. Thanks Laura.'' He sank into his chair and leaned back, feeling the tension leave him. Well, not all the tension. Talking to Laura was never exactly relaxing.

''I'm sorry if I disturbed you,'' she said, sounding more nervous than ever. ''I probably shouldn't bother you at work.''

''No, not at all. I'm really pleased you rang.''

''Right, then, I'll—er—keep in touch.''

''Thanks, Laura. I'd appreciate that.'' Hell! She was about to hang up and he hadn't mentioned dinner.

''Maybe tonight the girls can ring you at home to have a chat?'' she suggested.

''OK,'' he said slowly, while his mind raced. His chances of swinging the conversation to dinner were dwindling. Her suggestion didn't sound at all promising. It was Laura's way of telling him not to bother coming around this evening. He cleared his throat. ''A telephone chat with the girls would be—*nice*.''

"Unless, of course, you'd like to come to my place and see them."

Nick sat up straight. "Is that an invitation?"

"I—I guess so," she said, sounding doubtful. Then she laughed nervously. "Yes, it's an invitation."

"Well, I'd love to see the girls," he told her. "Maybe I could bring dinner."

"Oh?" She sounded surprised, almost shocked. "I—I thought that if you came and read the girls a bedtime story I could cook dinner. I could feed them something simple first and then rustle up something more—more adult for us."

Before he could interrupt, she hurried on anxiously. "What do you like? I was thinking about Thai-style fish. Maybe coral trout—or—um..." There was a pause and Nick heard the slight rustle of pages. "Or maybe you'd prefer something like wild mushroom risotto?"

With a sudden grin, Nick opened the magazine he'd just bought. Steamed coral trout and wild mushroom risotto. "Either of those dishes sound excellent," he told her. "My favourites."

"Your *favourites?* Really?" There was an edge of panic in Laura's voice. "Well, don't expect too much—I'm not a brilliant cook."

"Then let's make a slight change in the game plan," Nick suggested quickly, surprised at how easily the cards were falling his way. "I'll bring the ingredients and do the cooking while you read the girls their stories. They're bored with my stories anyhow."

There was a long silence on the other end of the line. "Are you sure you want to cook?"

"Steamed coral trout? You bet."

"I can give you a list of ingredients."

"I doubt that's necessary. I can manage."

"You know what to get?"

"Let me guess." He held up the magazine in front of him. "For the coral trout, I'll need soy sauce, oyster sauce, coriander roots, fresh ginger... Am I on the right track?"

"Amazingly accurate," she murmured.

"It's a cinch for a kitchen genius."

"Oh, for heaven's sake," Laura responded with more like her usual snap. "Then please don't let me stand in your way. By all means, you do the cooking."

"My pleasure."

CHAPTER NINE

HAVING their Daddy in the house seriously disrupted the girls' usual bedtime routine, and when Laura eventually managed to bustle them off to their room for stories they took even longer than ever to settle.

By the time she headed back out into the kitchen Nick had their meal pretty much under control.

He was standing at her stove and she paused to admire the picture he made. Unmistakable masculinity—black hair, grey eyes, blue jeans and navy shirt—surrounded by the feminine buttercup-yellow of her walls and cupboards.

She had a sneaking feeling she could get used to a sight like that in her kitchen. Not that Nick was planning on hanging around.

Not yet, anyway.

But if Susie's advice was right...

On the bench beside him stood a bottle of wine already opened and two glasses.

199

"You deserve a drink," he said with a grin. "This is a light wine designed to prepare your taste buds for what's to come."

For what's to come!

Laura's mouth went desert-dry and she tried to wet her lips with her tongue. It didn't work. She ran her damp hands nervously down the outside of her trousers. Dry mouth, damp hands, quaking heart: she was a mess. *Nick had no idea what was to come.* He didn't have a clue that she was planning to seduce him.

Planning was the operative word. As yet, she didn't have the foggiest idea how she was actually going to pull off such a plan.

Yikes! Just thinking about the expression on Nick's face and what he would say or do when she told him she'd changed her mind lowered her communication skills to the level of a chimpanzee's. How did you tell a man that you suddenly wanted him to stay for more than a meal?

My days as a prude are over? I just happened to turn into a sex beast overnight?

Oh, help! It was better not to think about it. When the time came, she would find the words.

Normally she didn't drink alcohol, but when Nick handed her a glass she took it. She would need some extra courage this evening. She clutched it against her chest as she looked into the pan he was working at. "So you decided on the risotto?"

"It was more a case of risotto chose me," he replied. "No coral trout in the shops at the moment—but plenty of wild mushrooms."

She sniffed appreciatively. "Smells great. It looks—" She paused, frowning. "That's amazing. It looks just like the picture I saw today in a magazine. Good grief, Nick, it looks almost exactly like a recipe I'd been thinking about using."

"Fancy that," he said with a strange little smile. "Maybe we've got something in common after all." He raised his glass to clink it against hers. "Cheers."

"Cheers," she repeated.

"Let's drink to finding what else we have in common, Laura."

"Yes," Laura whispered, and she tried not think about the after-dinner activity she planned to share with Nick. Just in time, she remembered not to gulp her wine.

It tasted mellow and very pleasant, but she could feel the effects of the chilled Chardonnay lighting her veins almost immediately. Best to keep her wits about her. She set the glass aside and busied herself by clearing away the remnants of the girls' meal and resetting the kitchen table with fresh place mats and serviettes.

Her cottage was too tiny to have a separate dining room, so they had to eat in the kitchen. It wasn't really practical to dim the lights, but she lit a jasmine-scented candle in the hope that it would create some atmosphere. Maybe the right atmosphere would help her to feel braver.

"I'd say this is ready," Nick reported.

He dished up the meal with easy, competent flourishes, while Laura took a seat and fiddled with the stem of her wine glass.

She figured that even if they dined at a refined pace it couldn't take them any more than fifteen or twenty minutes to actually eat this risotto. And then maybe there would be coffee, but after last night's little episode Nick would probably feel compelled to leave.

That meant she didn't have very long to develop the right mood for telling him about— her *change of heart.*

Butterflies danced in her chest. She would have to start laying some groundwork immediately. It was time to let Nick know she wasn't quite so inexperienced with men as he suspected.

Laura lifted her fork and sampled her food. "Mmm, delicious," she said sincerely. And then she decided it was best to jump in at the deep end.

She took a quick sip of wine. "I haven't dined in this kitchen alone with a man since— since Oliver," she said, with what felt like a very wobbly smile.

Nick's fork froze midway to his mouth. "And how long would that be?"

Laura could tell by the tight-lipped way he asked that it was only one of a host of questions he would have liked to fire at her, so she decided to get everything off her chest in a rush. ''It's five years since Oliver left. He used to come around for—for dinner twice a week. Most weeks anyhow.''

''Oliver was a colleague?'' Nick asked doubtfully.

''Oh, no. *No,* he was a— He was someone I met at a conference. He sold books. Actually, he represented quite a big publishing company. He was my boyfriend. Amazingly charming.''

''I see.''

''But that's not important,'' Laura hastened to explain.

Nick's wary eyes considered her. ''So what is important about Oliver besides his amazing charm and book-selling skills?''

''It's just that his visits were never quite like this. They weren't cosy.''

Nick didn't comment.

''He never cooked for me and he'd always be in such a hurry.''

''So the astonishing charm didn't last?'' He smiled faintly.

''He would come dashing in from work and he'd be so anxious to get into bed he would bolt down the meal I'd spent ages preparing. And he'd hardly notice if it was pepperoni pizza or coq au vin.''

She glanced at Nick to see how he was reacting, but his expression was too stony to interpret.

''Of course, he never offered to cook for me, and he never took me *out* to dinner.''

Nick grunted something incomprehensible.

''I know *now* why we never dined out. He was frightened of meeting someone he knew. Someone who knew he was *married*.''

She took a quick taste of the risotto. ''Oh, Nick, this is *really* delicious.'' Then she heard Nick's splutter and looked up at him. ''What's the matter?''

He didn't speak, but just sat there looking stony. No, she realised, he'd gone beyond stony—Nick looked stunned.

''I've shocked you,'' she said.

''Yes. I think you have.''

''I'm sorry, Nick.''

''Don't apologise. I'm just assimilating the facts. Let me see. Oliver, of the fantastic charm and incredible book-selling ability, but with an

appalling appreciation for fine food, used to
race you off to the bedroom although he was
married?''

His steely grey eyes held hers. ''It's rather
a lot to take in. Especially coming from Laura
Goodman.''

''I had to say it all in a rush like that or I
wouldn't have got it out.''

''I see. So you had to get it out. You thought
it was vital for me to know you had an affair
with a married man?''

Laura winced. ''Yes.''

Nick placed his knife and fork very delib-
erately on his plate and folded his arms across
his chest. ''Tell me why.''

''*Why?*''

''Why did you feel compelled to offload this
information?''

He was looking at her so fiercely that Laura
had to lower her eyes. ''I wanted you to understand,'' she told the plate in front of her.
''I felt so dreadful. I didn't know Oliver was
married. I thought he was going to marry *me*.
I wanted to die when I found out he had a wife
and three little boys.''

For a moment his voice gentled as he said, "That must have been a terrible discovery."

Laura looked up. "If there's a word that means worse than terrible, that's how I felt."

Nick nodded and took a slow sip of wine.

She downed some of her own wine. This was the hardest part. Nick would expect her to explain *exactly* why it was important for him to understand about Oliver.

Oh, dear. Now she had to make links between her past and what she hoped would be her future. She had to find a way to give him the green light to make love to her. After the king-sized fuss she'd made last night.

She'd hurried too quickly through her explanations. They were supposed to be finishing their meal by the time she got to this point, but Nick still had quite a lot of food on his plate.

She took a deep breath. "You see, Nick, you and I do have plenty in common. In different ways, we are both affected by our past relationships. You explained to me how you feel about Miranda and why you can't commit. I wanted to explain about Oliver and why I've been reluctant to—to agree to a casual relationship—'' She stopped as a movement in the doorway distracted her.

Oh, Lord! Felicity was standing there, looking tiny and tousled in her crumpled nightdress. She was clutching her teddy bear.

How long had she been listening?

''Fliss, what do you want?'' Nick asked quickly, and Laura heard the edge of impatience in his tone.

''A drink of water,'' the child said solemnly.

''OK. You go back to bed. I'll bring it into you.'' He jumped up and filled a tumbler at the sink. As he passed Laura on the way to the bedroom he rolled his eyes to the ceiling.

Nick's mind was still reeling from the conversation in the kitchen as he sat on the edge of the little white bed and met the shining directness in his daughter's gaze.

''Daddy, do you like Laura?'' Felicity asked as she nestled back into bed and Nick tucked the sheets up under her chin.

Right now, his feelings about Laura were as clear as mud. "Yes, Fliss," he said. "I like her."

Like a Jack-in-the-box, Felicity sat straight up again and crossed her chubby arms over her little chest. Her dark brows drew low as she looked up at Nick sternly. "But, Daddy, do you *really* like her?" Serious grey eyes, so like his own, challenged him.

But Nick didn't spend his days asking leading questions in court simply to come home and be caught out by his five-year-old daughter. He gave her tummy a tickle as he sent her question straight back. "What about you, Fliss, do *you* really like Laura?"

Her answer was spontaneous. "Oh, yes, Daddy, I do. I *love* Laura."

He dropped a kiss on her soft, rosy cheek and suppressed a sigh. "That's good, moppet," he whispered, thinking how easy it was for Fliss to talk about *love*. The word slipped off her tongue without the slightest hesitation.

But she was talking about the no-strings love of a child. Pure, unselfish love. Unstoppable, undemanding, unfettered love.

So different from the mess adults made of it.

For a moment he felt a stab of nostalgia for the carefree days of his childhood. The love between adults was so complex.

It could stop without warning. It was extremely demanding. And it came with baggage and chains attached.

As he rose again and prepared to leave the room he fancied he caught a slight movement from Kate's bed, but when he turned her way she was lying very still with her eyes closed.

He walked back down the passage to the kitchen, reflecting that three females were more than a match for one mere male. *And, yes, Fliss,* he thought when he saw Laura standing near the microwave, *I like Laura— especially the way she looks.*

She was wearing a loose sleeveless top in a rich cream colour that made the deep cherry of her hair look more luxurious and beautiful than ever. The top was knitted and kitten-soft. She looked so *touchable.*

How could he not *like* the subtle sway of her breasts beneath that soft creamy knit as she moved? And as for the way the slim-fitting trousers hugged the delicious curve of her behind—he found it incredibly difficult not to stare.

She said, ''I thought I'd zap your meal for you. It would be a shame to let it grow cold.''

''Thanks.'' He nodded as he sat down again and refilled their wine glasses.

Laura smiled at him shyly and placed his heated food in front of him. He wasn't sure if he smiled back, he was still coming to terms with the jolting physical impact her beauty always had on him.

Added to that, he was still assimilating Laura's news.

As they ate in uncomfortable silence Nick mused over what she had told him. A woman like Laura would be devastated to discover she'd been making love to someone else's husband. It was probably enough to scare her off men for good. *For at least five years.*

Hang on! He sat bolt upright as he remembered the last thing she'd said. *I wanted to explain why I've been reluctant to agree to a casual relationship.* Nick felt his breathing constrict. He fiddled with his collar, which felt uncomfortably tight, but realised he wasn't wearing a tie.

Reluctant, she'd said. OK. Reluctant meant unwilling, but it also implied hesitation rather than absolute refusal. So, did that mean she was no longer totally rejecting the idea of a casual affair?

''Felicity's OK?'' Laura asked.

''Er—yes, the little monkey has always been a bit of an attention-seeker,'' he said, relieved to sidetrack into safer subjects than Laura's attitude to sex.

''She's developing a very strong personality.''

''She might be a handful when she hits the teen years.'' He smiled at her. ''What were you like as a teenager?''

''Oh, what do you think?''

''Good as gold.''

She grinned self-consciously. ''Yes. I worked hard at school. Lived a quiet life. Didn't do anything to shock my parents.'' Over the top of her wine glass, her blue gaze met his. ''And what about you?''

He shrugged. "I lived up north on the Atherton Tableland. You know how it is in the bush. We had a lot of freedom. Rob and I used to get up to plenty of mischief."

"When did you meet Miranda?"

"She was there, too. We started dating when we were sixteen."

"Childhood sweethearts," Laura said softly. "So you and Rob and Miranda all grew up together?"

"Yes. And we all left the north together, when we came to university here in Brisbane."

Laura had finished her meal. She looked suddenly nervous as she held her wine glass stiffly in front of her.

Nick felt edgy too. He suspected she was going to swing the conversation back to that *other* subject. *Sex.* Not that he usually shied away from that topic, but this was *Laura*. After last night's rejection, talking about sex with her wasn't exactly a boost to the ego.

"Nick, I've changed my mind," she said suddenly.

It was there again. That trouble he had earlier with his breathing. ''Dare I ask just exactly what you've changed your mind about?''

''About us.'' An incredible pink tide rose from her neck and up her cheeks till it reached her hair line. ''I think you're right. I think we need to work out what's really going on between us. I would like to—'' She swallowed some wine. ''I think perhaps we should make love.''

''Daddy.''

Nick whipped around in the direction of the girlish voice. This time it was Kate, standing in the doorway in her nightgown. ''Kate, for heaven's sake!'' he exploded.

''I'm thirsty, too,'' she whispered, looking timid, as if she wished she'd never ventured out.

Nick jumped to his feet, strode towards the sink, filled a glass and thrust it rather roughly towards his daughter. He couldn't believe her sense of timing. ''I don't want to hear another peep from you girls. Do you understand?''

''Yes, Daddy,'' she said meekly.

He walked with Kate back to her room and watched as she drank some of the water and then climbed into bed. Felicity was lying in the other bed with her eyes squeezed tightly shut. Too tightly shut. Nick could tell that the naughty little muffin was feigning sleep.

"I'm disappointed with you girls," he told them. "Laura is very kindly looking after you while I'm—while I'm *busy* and you should be helping her by being good and going to sleep."

What a joke! Nick thought. Next minute the girls would be asking why he was here at Laura's place every night if he was supposed to be so busy.

He was relieved to hear replies of "Yes, Daddy," from both his daughters. His heart melted as it always did and he gave them both hugs.

Kate was looking up at him with big brown eyes that peeped from beneath her fringe. "We promise we won't interrupt you any more," she said.

"We was just checkin' on you," Felicity told him.

"Checking on me?"

"Yes. We wanted to make sure you ki—"

"Fliss!" hissed Kate. "Shut up." She glared across to the other bed.

"Oops—sorry."

Puzzled, Nick gave both girls another warning that he didn't want to see them tonight, and walked out of the room. But, from just beyond the doorway, he heard Felicity's voice.

"We should have told him he *has* to kiss Laura."

"No, we shouldn't," came Kate's loudly whispered reply. "I rang Grandma this afternoon and she said we have to let nature take its course."

"What does that mean?"

"I think it means he'll kiss her when the time is right. Maybe he has to wait till he feels like it."

"I don't think he ever will," sighed Felicity. "I think he doesn't understand that grown-up ladies like kissing."

In the darkened passage, Nick choked in disbelief. What on earth had his mother-in-law and his daughters been discussing? He wasn't sure if the emotion he swallowed was a desperate urge to cry out with rage or to chuckle wildly.

He spoke through the darkness in his sternest voice. "Girls, I don't want to hear any more talking."

There was a lengthy silence after that and, finally satisfied, he walked back down the passage, shaking his head. *Now his mother-in-law was involved!*

There were *far* too many females in his life!

When he reached the kitchen, he grabbed up his wine glass and took a deep swig. "I've made the girls promise to stay in bed." He remained standing beside the table.

Laura nodded, looking embarrassed.

"Now, where were we?" Nick continued as he tried to ignore the disturbing way his body throbbed as he looked at her. "Were you actually saying what I thought you were saying?"

She covered her face with her hands. "Do you think Kate understood?"

He frowned. "I doubt it. I'm not even sure if I heard you correctly myself."

Setting his glass aside, he reached down and drew her hands away from her face. "At least I don't think we'll be disturbed by the girls again tonight."

When she looked up at him, her blue eyes were filled with a bewildering mixture of emotions. She left her hands in his grasp as she rose and stood beside him. "We should go to my room," she said softly, so softly he only just caught the words.

Nick's body leapt at her suggestion. "You sure you want to?" he whispered.

One eyebrow rose. "Would I be suggesting it if I didn't want to?"

Without saying another word she withdrew her hands from his, turned, and walked away from him, moving silently down the carpeted passage, past the girls' closed door, past the bathroom, to her room. In the doorway she paused and looked back at him over her shoulder.

For a moment she stood there, looking slender and lovely and infinitely vulnerable and then she disappeared inside.

Nick followed.

How could he not follow?

This moment was something out of his dreams.

Since he'd met Laura, she'd haunted his nights with her soft, blue-eyed beauty. All through the meal he'd thought about lifting off that cream sweater.

So many times he'd fantasised about those pale, perfect shoulders of hers and how the rest of her skin would be the same.

White as the moon.

Round and womanly soft.

Warm with wanting—like her mouth whenever he'd kissed her.

He entered her room and shut the door firmly behind him. There was a key in the lock and he turned it. He nodded towards the door and tried to crack a grin. "We don't want to share this with anyone."

Her bedroom wasn't frilly, as he'd expected. Not a glimpse of virginal white anywhere. Not that he was actually trying to take in details. He wasn't looking at anything except Laura.

But she was standing beside her bed and he couldn't avoid seeing it in the soft lamplight.

Her bed looked sensational—as if it was designed for a night of wild romping. A generously fat quilt in two-tone shades of antique gold and purple covered the entire bed and scattered on top of this was a decadent pile of king-sized pillows in vibrantly coloured silks.

The urge to sweep Laura into his arms and to tumble, with her long, pale legs wrapped around him, into all that richly coloured softness and silk was too much.

Nick stepped towards her.

Her quiet voice halted him. "I understand this will be a one-night stand."

"Uh-huh."

"No complications, no expectations. The way you want it."

"Sure."

"Just sex…"

Just sex. Sure, that was what he wanted.

Yes. He wanted to peel those clothes away from her and find her round, rosy tipped breasts and softly curving hips. He wanted to drive this woman wild. He wanted to hear her make those hungry little noises again as he kissed her. All over.

Tonight she'd learn what fun a man and a woman could have without all the clutter of emotional baggage, and he was damn sure he could be an improvement on old Oliver.

She stood very still, looking up at him, and her big eyes were huge in her delicate, pale face.

Just sex.

He wanted her so badly he was trembling. He could already sense the petal softness of her lips and his breath caught as he imagined the way they would open to him so he could taste the sweet, moist heat of her mouth.

Her enticing perfume fragranced the air all around him and he wondered if she'd sprinkled it on the sheets. The thought that she'd prepared her bed for him was so erotic.

Just sex.

Great!

She was offering herself to him.

His heart pounded and he fancied hers did too. Any second now he would lose himself in Laura Goodman. The fever of his anticipation was unbearable.

Just sex. This was going to be *so* good.

So what the hell was the matter with him?

Why was he stuffing around like a pubescent walking hormone, as if he didn't have a clue what to do?

Nick groaned.

"What's the matter?" Laura whispered.

"Laura, I'm not sure you really want this."

"How could you know what I want?" She sounded distressed.

Nick's throat was so choked up it was hard to speak. "You told me most definitely last night."

"I—I've rethought the situation."

"But are you sure?" Nick could hardly believe that question had come out of his mouth.

If word got out…

He could imagine the inter-office memo. *Gorgeous woman offers herself to Nick Farrell and is subsequently forced to stand waiting while he runs a lie-detector test past her.*

What the hell was wrong with him?

All the lady wanted was sex. *Just sex.* When had that become a problem?

Right now.

Because…because if he had sex with Laura she would start thinking about love. He was worried that she would want to own him in some way.

No, he wasn't!

Nick gulped. That was only half of the problem.

The real problem was *his*.

He was standing here in Laura Goodman's bedroom, with her sensational, willing body just inches from his and he was stalling. And the real reason was that he'd copped a painful kick in the guts. A bachelor's revelation.

He suddenly *knew* that touching and kissing and taking Laura couldn't possibly be *just sex*…because she wasn't just any woman.

She was Laura. She was incredibly kind and generous and way too sweet and beautiful. If he was to take her in his arms, to taste her, to give her pleasure and to join his body intimately with hers—he wouldn't be *just having sex!*

He would be making *love*.

To *Laura*.

And that was a problem. Chances were that after just one night he might fall completely *in love* with the woman.

And he couldn't risk that.

He didn't dare risk falling in love.

What a mess! Nick felt ill. This was physical and mental torture of the very worst kind.

"Nick, I didn't expect to have to show you what to do. I'm the one whose memory is rusty." Laura's face crumpled a little as she tried to smile. "Remember? I haven't done this for five years."

Oh, hell! He was a coward and she was being brave and gutsy about it. Trying to make a joke.

And her courage was killing him.

CHAPTER TEN

LAURA felt sick.

Nick was standing in the middle of her bedroom looking as if he wanted to escape. Heavens, that was usually her role. It was the very last thing she'd expected from him. What had she done wrong?

He was actually stepping away from her and looking at her sternly, the same way he'd looked at Kate when she'd come to the kitchen for a glass of water.

"This is a mistake," he said.

She felt her knees give way. "This is *very* embarrassing."

"I know. I'm sorry."

He was *sorry?* Oh, that was a good one! Minutes, maybe only seconds ago, Nick had been anything but sorry. He'd definitely been about to take her to bed. There was no mistaking the dark heat of desire in his eyes.

It was the hungry look of a man about to get laid.

And she'd been about to give thanks for Nick Farrell, God's gift to women.

But now...

Now...he was standing in front of her, looking as if the thought of touching her was as unpleasant as petting a redback spider.

And that was unbearably embarrassing.

She'd lured him into her room. She'd planned seduction down to the last detail. *For heaven's sake!* She'd even rushed out at lunch time and spent a fortune on new sheets and pillows and a glamorous quilt for her bed. But somehow, at the last minute, she'd managed to turn Nick off.

"What's wrong?" she whispered. "I'm not wearing a danger sign, am I?"

He looked miserable. "You should be."

"Why? I'm too much of a geek?"

"Of course not, Laura."

"Did I fail a random breath test?"

"Don't be silly." He lifted a hand to his forehead and rubbed it as if his head ached.

"If there was any kind of test, you passed it with flying colours."

"I don't get it."

His mouth twitched into a sad smile. "There isn't a lot to get. Look, this is nothing to do with whether or not you're a desirable woman. It's to do with me."

"I see." There was a solid block of silence while she thought about that. "I thought a casual fling was what you wanted."

"Yeah." Nick looked at the door. "Listen, I'd better go."

She shrugged helplessly. Miserably. There was absolutely nothing she would do to try to keep him from leaving. Her disappointment and embarrassment were painful in the extreme, but she would do her darned best not to show Nick how she felt. Just the same, as he walked towards the door she couldn't help muttering, "Some daredevil."

He turned. "I beg your pardon?"

"I—I don't think you're much of a daredevil."

"When have I ever been a daredevil?"

"Oh, come on, Nick, if someone had *dared* you to make love to me we wouldn't still be standing here talking."

He frowned. "You really think I'm that shallow?"

Laura dropped her gaze. "It seems to me you will do just about anything for a dare."

"Who told you that?"

"I've seen it for myself. The clown stint at the hospital. Susie's party. You could strip for a room full of women—"

She had a sudden vision of Nick at Susie's party—with his cheeky grin and his muscles rippling as he swung his T-shirt over his head. She wanted to cry.

What had happened to the bold and confident Nick, the guy who'd dared her to kiss him that night? What had happened to the man who'd stood in this cottage just last night trying to persuade her into this very bed?

Was this really the same man who'd urged her to throw aside her silly inhibitions?

What had gone so wrong?

When she looked up again, his dark grey eyes held a world of regret and Laura wasn't sure how she managed not to cry.

He spoke softly. "That room full of women at Susie's party wasn't nearly as risky as this room with just one real princess, Laura."

As he said that his eyes shimmered.

And as she stood there seeing the damp gleam in his eyes, she knew. Oh, she knew. She read the truth. "You're frightened of what this might lead to."

His smile was bleak. "You got it."

He didn't *dare* to risk his emotions. Tears burned in Laura's throat. Didn't Nick realise how unfair and cruel this was? She sniffed, determined not to cry.

"Nick, it's all very well for you to say no, but you've just been playing games with me." She was amazed by her nerve. Amazed that by some strange exchange of energies his fear was giving her courage.

"I'm sorry if it seems that way," he said.

"Of course that's how it seems. You've paid me compliments. You've been saying all these pushy things about wanting me. And when I finally weaken—when I do respond— you reject me.''

''Laura, please—''

''How unfair is that?''

He frowned, but didn't answer.

Laura felt suddenly empty. Drained. She couldn't take any more of this. She crossed the room, wrenched the key in the lock and hauled the door open for him to leave.

She was proud that her voice didn't shake as she said coldly, ''I think there's nothing more to be said but goodnight.''

He nodded grimly. ''Goodnight, Laura.''

''Remember to lock the back door.''

''Of course.''

Just before he left her bedroom, he paused and looked down at her with dark, disturbed eyes. ''I shouldn't keep imposing on you like this. I'll see if I can find somewhere else for the girls to stay.''

Laura almost groaned. ''I've said it doesn't matter, but—by all means do as you wish.''

He nodded and she clung to the door frame for support as he stepped out of the room. But, as he brushed passed her his arm touched her breast. It was just a whisper of sensation, but a fiery flash of longing electrified Laura and she heard the harsh rush of Nick's in-drawn breath.

He hesitated.

She stopped breathing. It was as if her blood stood still in her veins for one, two, three shuddering, indecisive heartbeats.

Their eyes met and Laura nearly sobbed aloud at the longing and the sadness she saw in Nick's beautiful face.

But then he jerked his gaze away and kept on going out of her house.

This time Laura didn't cry when Nick left. She was too paralysed. For ages she stood numb and dazed, without moving. Finally she turned and stared at her room, and the gloriously sumptuous bed seemed to mock her.

The stupid part was, she thought miserably, she could tell he didn't really want to reject her. It was because he was scared of taking risks with his emotions. Nick was frightened of falling in love with her.

She crossed the floor and flopped down onto her bed, sinking miserably into the soft, luxurious quilt, and she lay there, with one hand restlessly stroking the silky fabric, while a cold, unfriendly moon leaned in through her window to taunt her.

She had to agree with Nick that falling in love *was* a scary concept.

Incredibly scary.

She understood that now.

There were so many things she was learning tonight. And one of them was that at some time in the past week, when she wasn't even trying, she'd fallen totally, no-doubt-about-it in love with Nick Farrell.

She couldn't pinpoint when it had happened, maybe it had been there from the moment she first saw him, but she knew with an awful certainty that it was so.

She had never felt this deeply about Oliver. Her body ached with her need for Nick. But it wasn't just a physical ache. She loved everything about the man. His smile, his voice…every cell in his body. The way he fathered his daughters. She hadn't known him very long, but already she couldn't imagine her life without him.

So she understood Nick's fear. Recognising that kind of love was an alarming process.

Knowing she loved him and watching him walk away from her this evening had been the most frightening experience of her life.

Complete emotional and physical exhaustion ensured that she slept surprisingly well, but when Laura woke next morning in her luxurious, sexy and ridiculously expensive bed, her first thoughts were of Nick.

She sank back into her pillow with a groan of dismay as her mind replayed in vivid detail the ordeal of the night and the embarrassing sight of his stiff, proud back as he walked away from her.

And she might have lain there for some time, wallowing in self-pity, if sounds of giggling, girlish laughter hadn't drifted down the hall from the kitchen. Kate and Felicity were up already.

Laura swung her legs out of bed, grateful for the blessed distraction of the busy morning rush required to organise the girls' breakfast and get them ready for school.

By the time she dropped them off at the school's main door she was feeling much better. She decided it was one of life's little ironies that Nick's lively, loving daughters could provide an antidote to the hurt their father caused her.

Luckily, it was a busy day in the library as well, and she could *almost* keep thoughts of Nick in the background. But shortly after lunch she answered the phone and heard his familiar baritone.

"Good afternoon, Laura."

The sickening knot of despair she'd been trying to ignore tightened in her stomach. "Hello, Nick."

"I won't keep you long. I just wanted to let you know I've been able to make alternative arrangements for the girls."

Laura jammed a fist against her lips to hold back a protest.

"We've been imposing on you for too long."

She closed her eyes. "I've never minded."

"I know you say that, Laura, and you're very kind—"

"I mean it. I've really enjoyed having the girls."

"Yes," Nick said softly.

"But maybe—" Laura's hands shook as she gripped the receiver. "But maybe it would be better if we—" Her throat closed over and she didn't think she could continue. She coughed. "I can understand that the whole situation might be getting too complicated."

"My dad's tests are completed and he's been given the all-clear so he and Mum are very keen to see the girls. I'm going to send them up there till this whole business with the phone calls and the stalking settles."

"I guess that's sensible."

"It's the only way, Laura. Stokes is bound to find out about you sooner or later. I've booked plane tickets to Cairns for this evening."

"I see." *So soon?* He really was anxious to be clear of her.

"The airline people have been very understanding. A flight attendant will keep a watchful eye on Kate and Fliss."

Laura nodded. "It will be a big adventure for them." She was so glad Nick couldn't see the way she was trembling. She would miss Kate and Felicity, but the fact that they were leaving wasn't what was making her feel so shaky and ill. She was glad they could get away to somewhere right out of Brisbane. Somewhere safe.

No, that wasn't what upset her.

It was Nick and the way he sounded so calm and definite today, so confident and in charge once more. The uncertain, hesitant man who'd faced her last night was a different person now that he'd found a way to distance himself and his daughters from her.

Knowing that hurt. But the last thing Laura wanted was for Nick to realise how miserable he made her feel. She struggled to concentrate on practical details. "When are you going to let the girls know about your new plans?"

"That's a problem," Nick admitted. "I'm caught up here for the next few hours."

"Did you want me to tell them when I pick them up this afternoon?"

"Would you mind, Laura? I doubt they'll object to a sudden trip to their grandparents' place," he added. "They love it up there."

She swiped at her eyes with a tissue. "So you'll pack their things before you come over to collect them?"

"Yes." There was a slight pause. "I'll need to pick them up around six-thirty."

Laura could picture how it would be. Nick's car would speed into her driveway and his daughters would jump into it, delighted at the thought of a sudden, unexpected adventure.

In a matter of minutes they would be gone. All three of them. Her part in their lives would be over.

Her throat tightened painfully and she had to take a deep breath before she could speak. "Sure. That'll be OK. I'll just collect the girls from school as usual."

"Thanks, Laura." After a pause he added, "You're a good sport, you know."

"Of course I am. I'm a Goodman." Laura dropped the receiver and sagged forward onto the desk.

She was a good sport.

Her head slumped onto her arms. Nick had convinced himself she meant no more than one of his mates, she thought bitterly. Of course Nick had never promised her anything, not even friendship. She could only blame herself for this wretchedness she felt. She and Nick Farrell were two people whose lives had crossed briefly and she'd been able to help him out.

And now he thought she was a sport. A good egg.

No more, no less.

The rest—the kisses, the flirtation, the strong sense of connection and attraction? Her undisciplined, wild imagination had blown all that out of proportion.

But she couldn't help her feelings. No matter how hard she tried to think sensibly, she remained awash with pain and it was all because she had made the mistake Nick had been so careful to avoid. She'd fallen in love.

And this horrible sense of loneliness, this unbearable pain was the result. No wonder Nick had been so cautious.

*   *   *

"Are you coming, too?" Felicity asked as soon as Laura collected the girls from school and told them their father's news.

"Oh, no, dear. I have to stay here and work at the library."

"What about Daddy?"

"He has to keep working, too."

Kate chimed in. "Will Daddy still visit you if we're at Granny's?"

Laura frowned. "I don't think so," she said carefully, wondering just what was going on in the little girl's mind.

When her reply was followed by a long silence in the back of the car, Laura asked, "It doesn't matter if your daddy and I don't see each other, does it?"

"Yes, it does!" Felicity cried emphatically, and to Laura's surprise the child sounded close to tears.

"Well, don't worry about us," Laura told her. "Just think about all the fun you're going to have with Granny and Grandpa."

They reached the library and two very solemn little girls climbed slowly out of Laura's car. She couldn't see any of their usual sparkle or eagerness. Laura sighed. This wasn't how they were supposed to react at all.

Felicity stood in front of Laura and looked up at her with steady grey eyes. ''Could you tell me if Daddy has kissed you yet?''

''Fliss!'' Kate glared, giving her sister a rough dig with her elbow.

''Has he?'' Felicity shouted, on the very edge of tears.

Stunned, Laura looked down at the little woebegone faces. ''Don't hurt your sister, Kate. I don't mind the question.'' She kept her voice steady as she asked, ''Do you want your daddy to kiss me?''

Both girls nodded.

Laura forced a smile. ''Why is kissing so important? A kiss doesn't really mean anything.''

''Oh, Laura,'' scolded Kate, ''don't you know anything? If a boy kisses you it means he loves you. Once Daddy kisses you, you can get married.''

''No,'' Laura protested weakly. ''It's not quite like that. Even if—even if we did kiss, we won't be getting married.''

"Yes, you will. I just know you will," came the definite reply. "So just make sure Daddy gets to kiss you soon."

And before Laura could explain the flaws in the girls' logic the two excited sisters rushed into the library, apparently very pleased that they had finally imparted this very important information.

Laura followed at a more subdued pace, wondering how on earth she could set them straight and still send them off happily on the plane this evening. Nick was right, she realised. There were all sorts of dangers in telling little girls the happily-ever-after endings in fairy tales.

At five, when the library closed, Laura drove the girls home to her place for the last time. At first when she noticed the driver in a black sedan travelling too closely behind her she was merely cranky with him. But when she pulled in at the greengrocers to buy some salad items his car stopped further up the street and she felt faint stirrings of alarm.

A sixth sense warned Laura not to leave the girls in the car while she dashed into the shop.

They all piled into Joe's Fruit and Veg, and when she came out again she looked back at the black car. It was still parked in the same place and its driver hadn't moved. She couldn't see his face but she could make out the bulky shape of a man sitting behind the steering wheel.

Hairs rose on the back of Laura's neck. She made sure Kate and Felicity had their seat belts fastened and were happily munching on the grapes the greengrocer had given them before she pulled out into the traffic, but her stomach was churning.

The other car pulled out at almost the same moment as Laura. When she looked in her rear-vision mirror she could see it prowling behind her once more. It was a new model that seemed to hug the road, and it looked lower and blacker and more malign than ever.

It isn't sinister, Laura told herself silently. *This is just a coincidence. Your depression is colouring your thinking. You're just giving into negativity.*

But, as a precaution, she decided to vary the pace of her driving. No matter what speed she changed to, the black car stayed right behind her.

Oh, no! A surge of panic shot from her stomach straight to her throat. She struggled to breathe. This *could* be the stalker, the man who'd threatened Nick and his family.

It seemed that somehow he'd found out about *her*.

Fear drenched Laura with sweat. Her palms were so slippery she could hardly grip the steering wheel. *Not now.* Surely the stalker hadn't found them now, not when Nick had a new safety plan worked out.

Frantically, she scanned the street ahead. She had grown up in this suburb and she knew every back lane and underpass. At the next corner she took a sharp turn left and, driving as fast as she dared, she kept turning left until she was back on the main road again.

This time she headed in the opposite direction, took another swift turn to dash under a railway bridge and then another quick turn or two, and the next time she checked her mirror, the black car was gone.

But it wasn't until she'd continued for five minutes without seeing the hated vehicle that she breathed a little more easily. She wondered if she should drive to a police station, but the procedures there would be time-consuming.

She glanced at her watch. In less than an hour Nick would be arriving to pick up the girls. Too long with the police and they might miss their flight.

She decided to continue home, but she still took a circuitous route and the whole way her hands were tense as they gripped the steering wheel. Her heart thumped crazily and her stomach churned. Where was the stalker? Would he turn up at her house?

She'd thrown him off the trail for the moment, but there was a chance he already knew where she lived. She imagined him breaking into her cottage and trying to abduct the girls. The thought made her tremble. She knew she couldn't risk that happening.

The safety of the girls was paramount.

Instead of parking in her driveway, she pulled up into a little lane at the back of her house.

''Why are we stopping here?'' came Kate's predictable question.

''Daddy's coming to pick you up soon. I wanted to leave a space for him in my drive-way,'' she told them.

Hurrying the surprised girls down a side lane between her cottage and her neighbours, Laura explained, ''Girls, I'm going to ask Mrs Powell, the lady next door, to look after you for a little while.''

''Why?'' asked Felicity.

''I—I'm expecting a visitor and I have some business to discuss with him. Don't worry, I'll come and get you very soon. You've met Mrs Powell and she's very nice.''

The urgency in her voice must have con-vinced them. For a minute they stood looking at her, frowning and confused, and then they happily let her take their hands and lead them to her neighbour's door.

Thankfully, Janet Powell was a kind, sen-sible woman, who minded her own business.

She didn't hesitate to welcome the girls and immediately won their hearts by switching on their favourite afternoon television pro-gramme.

"I'll be back in half an hour," Laura prom-ised.

Once inside her own cottage, she decided to ring Nick and headed for the phone in her kitchen. She took another deep breath, forcing herself to relax as she lifted the receiver to key in Nick's number.

Her fingers were pressing the third digit when she glanced across the street and froze.

Framed by her yellow gingham curtains, she could see the black car parked directly oppo-site her house. The driver was wearing dark glasses but she knew he was staring straight at her.

CHAPTER ELEVEN

NICK glanced at his watch. He still had plenty of time. All he had to do was snap the locks on the two suitcases he had packed for the girls, drive to Laura's to pick them up and they would make it to the airport comfortably.

It had been a great relief to find that his parents were free to take the girls now. Kate and Felicity would love a surprise trip to visit Granny and Grandpa. Of course they had loved being at Laura's, too...

Nick tried not to think about the way his daughters' fondness for Laura had reached hero-worshipping proportions. But, to his annoyance, it was a fact that was very difficult to ignore.

Damn it, he'd been unsuccessfully trying to put Laura Goodman out of his mind ever since he'd left her house last night.

For hours he'd lain wide awake, manfully trying not to think about her...but, in spite of

247

248 THE WEDDING DARE

his best efforts, visions of her had persisted in taunting him. He hadn't been able to block out the special light in her bright eyes or the burnished sheen of her hair.

Memories of her gentle smile had come to him again and again.

What he'd fought hardest not to think about was how she'd stood there beside her bed...looking devastatingly beautiful in the lamplight...looking heartbreakingly brave as she'd offered him a night with no complications, no expectations...

What he couldn't—*mustn't* dwell on was the cowardly haste with which he'd run away from that offer...

...or the reason he was still running away.

He stood in the middle of his daughters' bedroom, looking at the two little suitcases, one red, the other blue, and told himself that very soon he could get on with the rest of his life. But all he could picture was an endless stretch of boring nights and empty mornings.

His mobile phone beeped and he frowned as he took it from the inside breast pocket of his suit jacket.

"Farrell speaking."

"Nick, it's Laura. You haven't hired anyone to watch me, have you?"

The stark fear in her voice shot a chill spiralling down his spine. "No, I haven't."

"Well, someone's following me. He's here now."

"You mean Stokes? The stalker?"

"I—I think so.

"Where is he?"

"Sitting in his car across the road directly opposite my house. What should I do?"

Stashing both suitcases under one arm, Nick hurried through his house as he kept talking into the phone. "Stay there, Laura. Keep the house locked."

"Should I ring the police?"

"I'll look after that. The downtown boys know me." With his elbow, Nick managed to open his front door. "Did you get a good look at this bloke?"

"No," she groaned. "I was too shocked. And he's wearing dark glasses."

Nick tossed the suitcases onto the back seat of his car and his mind whirred as he began to reverse out of his garage. "What about the girls? Are they frightened?"

"No. They don't know anything about him. I've taken them by the back way to my neighbour's just in case he tries to get in here."

"Clever girl," Nick murmured. "What about you? Are you OK?"

"I will be when you get here."

"I'm already on my way. Now you stay well and truly hidden in the house."

"But it'll take you ages to get through the peak hour traffic."

"Hang in there. I'll find a short cut and I'll contact the police right now. There'll be someone with you soon. Your job is just to keep the house locked."

"OK."

"Take care, sweetheart."

"I will. Hurry, Nick. I need you."

As he depressed the disconnect button Nick found himself whispering, "And I need you, Laura," and he was startled to hear those words coming from his lips. But, next moment, he recognised that they were true. Blindingly, obviously true.

And he was desperately sorry that she hadn't heard them.

Clasping her hands together, Laura turned away from the phone and tried to think calmly about what she must do. It was such a relief to know that Kate and Felicity were next door, happily giggling at cartoons.

As she stood there, considering her options, she heard footsteps. Footsteps moving with menacing stealth along the brick path at the side of her tiny cottage. Sharp prickles of fear broke out all over her skin.

She dashed to the kitchen window and stared in horror through the darkening twilight. The car across the street was empty. Sickening panic gripped her, squeezing the air from her lungs.

Her heartbeats boomed as her ears strained to listen for more noises, but she couldn't hear anything outside. What was happening?

Where was he?

Her imagination threw up a hair-raising image of his dark, threatening figure leaping through a doorway to attack her. She clamped a hand to her mouth, only just holding back a scream. The last thing she wanted was to terrify the girls next door.

She heard a faint click somewhere and her desperate eyes swung to the hat-stand in her hallway. Her umbrella, a pretty floral affair but quite sturdy, was the only possible weapon. It would have to do.

Grabbing it, she stood, listening, alert to the slightest sound. There was a squeak and scrape that sounded like a window opening.

Oh, help, Laura prayed. *I don't know if I'm strong enough for this.* Her heart pounded and she felt ill. Her hands and legs were shaking. Everything was shaking. She wasn't at all sure she was breathing.

She tried to move, but her feet were glued to the floor boards.

What could she do? Nick was on his way, and presumably the police were too, but in the meantime... *If only they would get here soon!*

And then she knew he was inside. She heard a heavy thud as his feet dropped to the floor. Terror leapt in her throat. For too long, she stood shaking with her eyes shut, clutching her umbrella, her mind frozen.

I should get away. Out the front door!

Once the thought took shape, Laura could move again. She hurried down the passage towards her door. Behind her she heard heavy footsteps and harsh breathing.

He was too close!

With a cry of sheer terror, Laura spun around. She had a vague impression of a stumpy, balding man with a big nose. He was looking at her with a sickly, smug grin. ''Nick Farrell doesn't need you all to himself, Laura.''

She yelled at him and raised the umbrella high, like a gladiator wielding a sword. It made a satisfying crunch as it came down on his shoulder. She heard his exclamation of surprise, but she struck out wildly, hitting him again.

Then she grabbed the door knob, wrenched the door open and stumbled outside. Her heart raced fit to burst.

Her mind spun. The whacks from the umbrella were not enough to slow this fellow down for long. Hurrying blindly down her front path, she was sure of only one thing. She had to keep this man occupied. She had to keep on going—to lead him away from the girls at Mrs Powell's.

She scurried on down the tree-lined street, and behind her she heard the steady thump of her pursuer's footsteps. She told herself it was good that he was following her. She just had to keep him diverted until the police arrived.

But she doubted she could move any faster in the shoes she'd been wearing at work all day—just as she doubted that her heart could pump any harder. Surely her chest would explode soon?

A quick glance over one shoulder showed that the stalker was gaining on her.

She struggled to kick off her shoes. In bare feet she would be so much faster. She managed to send one shoe flying, but next moment she stumbled as the heel of her other shoe caved in beneath her, and she felt a rough hand slap at her arm as her pursuer reached out to grab at her.

*   *   *

Nick screeched to a halt behind the black sedan parked opposite Laura's and his headlights lit up its interior, showing him immediately that there was no one inside. He cursed loudly.

Where was Stokes? He glanced quickly at Laura's neat cottage. The front door was open, but the curtains were drawn in every room except the kitchen. On the footpath in front of her house lay a furled umbrella.

Sliding out of the driver's seat quickly, he was about to dash across to the house when movements down the street grabbed his attention.

Night was falling quickly but he could make out the form of a man running beneath the rows of spreading jacarandas that lined the street. He was gaining on a woman.

Dashing to the footpath, Nick squinted through the gathering dusk. Ahead of him, the woman seemed to be stumbling.

It had to be Laura. He could see the bright flame of her hair streaming behind her.

His breath came in grunts as he sped towards them. Keeping his eyes fixed ahead, Nick saw Laura struggling to kick off her shoes. The fellow chasing her was too damn close. Dread plunged and kicked in Nick's guts.

Laura was almost at the point where her street joined the main road now. Too far away.

Nick had been a top sprinter in his university days, but he doubted his chances of reaching her before her pursuer did.

"Laura!" he roared, not caring how much he disturbed the neighbourhood. Vaguely, he was aware of porch lights turning on as he thundered past neat suburban hedges and white picket fences. Only one thing mattered and that was getting to Laura before Stokes did.

Don't let her be hurt, his mind screamed. *Don't let anything happen to her. When I get to her, I won't ever let her go.*

As he gained on them he saw Laura turn to look back over her shoulder, and he could see the flash of despair in her beautiful face when she realised how very close her pursuer was.

Nick waved his arms above his head and yelled again, hoping she would see him, but she wasn't looking his way. Her focus was purely on the man so close to her now.

Horrified, Nick saw her make a sudden shift in direction, veering behind the trunk of a jac-aranda towards the road as if desperately trying to avoid capture.

Not the road, Laura. For God's sake, watch out!

He saw the stalker lunge onto the bitumen after her. A split second later, there was a flash of headlights and a sickening screech of brakes.

And as if everything was happening in slow motion, Nick's horrified eyes saw two figures in the ghastly glare of the yellow headlights.

He saw the impact as the car hit them, two bodies spinning in mid-air and then, like rag dolls, falling together into a crumpled heap.

CHAPTER TWELVE

"LAURA!"

A horrible, tormented cry broke from Nick's lips as his legs ate up the final few metres.

He could feel his heart shattering like glass, splintering into sharp, painful spikes. By the time he reached the huddle of bodies he was praying hard.

He dropped to his knees. Laura was spread-eagled on the hard, black road next to Stokes. She was very still...too still. Her hair streamed out across the bitumen like blood. Her eyes were closed and her face was deathly pale.

No, please no!

Nick groaned. *He'd* done this to her! He'd asked her to care for his girls and he'd placed her at risk!

Her legs were entangled with Stokes's. Her knees were badly grazed and one of her pursuer's thick arms was flung over her chest as if he was still trying to grab at her.

Blood from a wound on Stokes's shoulder was soaking into Laura's clothes.

A couple of purple jacaranda bells fluttered down from an overhead branch to land on her pale throat as if she were simply part of the road.

With shaking fingers, Nick picked the blossoms off her perfect skin and laid them gently aside. He was dimly aware of the driver of the car leaning against the door of her vehicle, sobbing and crying over and over... ''I didn't see them. I just didn't see them...''

From up and down the street, people were running out of houses, crowding closer.

''Oh, my goodness, it's Laura from number thirty-two,'' someone cried.

''I've rung 000. The ambulance and police are coming,'' a man's voice called.

''What could have happened?''

What happened, Nick thought bitterly, was that this sweetheart had been trying to defend Kate and Felicity as bravely as any mother!

And this was the thanks she got.

Shaking with horror, he leant his ear close to her mouth and tried to sense the soft hush of her breath, but his own breathing was so frantic he couldn't possibly feel hers.

Desperately, he stared at her chest. Was it rising and falling? *Oh, please let her be breathing!* Why couldn't he think straight? What should he do?

God help him, all he could think of was how Laura had offered him her love and he'd rejected it as if it meant no more than the offer of a cup of coffee.

How could he have been so stupid?

Now it was too late.

Please, don't let it be too late!

A police car screeched to a halt and a policewoman pushed her way through the crowd. She knelt on the bitumen beside him and, with the calm assurance of someone who knew exactly what she was doing, she examined Laura. "She's breathing and there's a good pulse," she said grimly, "so that's a start. But we shouldn't move her till the ambulance gets here."

As she leant forward to examine the other body Nick found himself clinging to those words… *"She's breathing and there's a good pulse."*

Somewhere in the distance, there was the moan of a siren. And then another.

"Laura, please be all right!" he whispered as the wailing sounds drew nearer. "Hang on, please. I've something important to tell you!"

For a moment, her eyes snapped open and his heart leapt as he saw a flash of that familiar stunning blue. "Laura?"

But, too soon, her eyelids flickered and closed again. It was as if the warm, comforting dark was beckoning and she preferred it there. Nick trembled. He wanted to weep.

He needed to sweep her into his arms and run with her to the hospital.

Next moment, with a blare of sirens and flashing lights, more police cars and ambulances arrived. Nick was shoved out of the way.

A police constable he didn't recognise blocked his view of Laura and fired questions that he didn't want to waste time answering. Who cared how the accident had happened?

That wasn't vital right now. Nick strained to watch what was happening to Laura.

The ambulance officers were asking her questions. He could see that her eyes were open again. He fancied she spoke a word or two...

She was being lifted onto a stretcher...

Nick waved both hands at the ambulance men. "Hey! I have to travel with her to the hospital!" he shouted, but no one took any notice.

Annoyed, he elbowed his way forward. *How could they ignore him?* He would have to explain...

Then he felt someone tugging at his coat sleeve. "Excuse me," a woman said, sounding anxious, "are you the father of the two little girls who are staying with Laura?"

His head jerked sideways and he stared at the woman stupidly.

"I think you'd better come with me," she said. "They'll be very upset by all this."

The only light came from a small lamp glowing softly on the far wall. Laura looked around the darkened room. She was in a bed with crisp white sheets.

There was a chart on the end of her bed, a plastic water jug on a table beside her. The grey linoleum on the floor was highly waxed and there was a tag on her wrist.

It was all so strangely familiar. She visited this hospital every week, but she'd never been a patient before.

It seemed like a dream. The whirling lights, the sirens…drifting in and out of sleep as she was wheeled on a trolley through endless corridors…

Voices, the continuous rise and fall of voices. Lights being shone in her eyes, fingers waved at her. Questions…too many questions.

She'd had some questions of her own. ''What happened? What's the matter with me?''

And for too long, the answers had been unsatisfactory. ''You've had a bump on the head.''

The events of the afternoon had been coming back to her in pieces. At first all she'd been able to remember was picking up the girls from school...taking them back to the library... Had that been today or yesterday?

And then...oh, help! It had come back with a jolt! She remembered running...and running and... *The stalker!*

Once she'd reached hospital she'd been taken to the X-ray department. She hadn't been able to get anyone to tell her how Kate and Felicity were. No one had known what she was talking about.

"You're a very lucky woman," a doctor finally informed her. "Not many people run in front of a moving vehicle and get away with a touch of concussion. But because you've been tired and confused we'll keep you here for observation for a day or so."

"What happened to the man who was chasing me?"

The doctor hesitated. "He's a lot worse off than you. It seems he caught up with you just at the point of collision and he took the brunt of the blow. That's why you managed to escape with so little injury."

"Where is he?"

"We have him in another ward. A police guard is waiting to question him, but he won't worry you any more."

He won't worry you any more... Laura let the doctor's words sink in. It was hard to accept that all hint of danger was gone, but the doctor had sounded quite certain...

Her mind kept wrestling with the horrifying narrowness of her escape. She sank back into her pillows with her eyes closed...

"Hi there." Nick's voice sounded from the doorway, low and husky, as if he were afraid of waking her.

Her eyes shot open, and next minute he was walking towards her. He looked good. His dark hair was falling softly forward and he was gazing at her with incredible tenderness. She felt the warm grasp of his hand closing around hers.

"How are you feeling?" he asked gently.

"I seem to be perfectly OK," she told him, trying to sound much calmer than she felt. "But I've been so worried about the girls. Did you get them to the airport on time?"

She tried to sit up, but the sudden movement made her head pound.

"The girls are fine, Laura," Nick reassured her, and she felt his hands pressing her shoulders gently back into the pillows. "They're with Heather. There's no need for them to go away now. And you're going to be fine, too. So don't worry about a thing. Just thank your guardian angel."

"You think I have one?"

"I'm sure you do and I'd like to shake his hand." Nick's smile was strange and wobbly. As he spoke he held her hands in both of his, squeezing them, caressing them, pressing his lips to them, and it felt so good that instead of insisting on more answers she relaxed.

He bent over her and she smelt the warm, spicy scent of his aftershave as his lips gently kissed her eyelids closed.

"That's *very* nice," she whispered. "No one's ever kissed me on the eyelids before. I think I like it."

"Has anyone kissed you here?" Nick murmured, brushing his mouth ever so lightly against her temple.

"No, I'm sure they haven't." Laura couldn't help smiling. Nick's kisses felt so careful. He was being so sweet. And yet so stirring. Her skin was humming to life.

Her whole body was stirring. She stretched, feeling deliciously happy. Warmth was spreading through her, making her want to move close against him...and to have him kiss her and touch her and hold her...

"Do you think I should try to kiss you better?" He was smiling as he lowered his head.

"Doctor's orders." Laura smiled back and his mouth took hers in a lingering, deep kiss. A Nick Farrell special. She lifted her arms to encircle his neck and hold him close.

Everything about Nick was so special. The way he sounded, the way he looked and the way he kissed. Especially the way he kissed.

Oh, yes. Most definitely she liked his kisses. She could drown in the sensation of that beautiful mouth lovingly locked with hers. How sensational it would be to keep him here for the rest of the night—or, better still, for ever.

"Laura," Nick whispered against her lips, "I want to tell you how much I—"

The sudden clump and squeak of sensible shoes marching over the waxed linoleum cut off his words. Someone stomped into the room.

Nick looked up and his face broke into a rueful grin. "Oh, hello, Sister. I was checking our patient's vital signs. Can you give us five minutes?"

"Certainly not." The unsmiling, middle-aged nurse was clearly short on good humour or sympathy. "This patient needs to be left in peace to get some *vital* rest."

Nick murmured close to Laura's ear, "That sounds like my marching orders."

Reluctantly, she released him. "You were going to tell me something."

He stood up and smiled softly. "I won't tell you now, it's private, but don't worry, it'll keep. I won't forget."

Dismissing Nick with a sniff, the nurse set about grabbing Laura's arm and taking her blood pressure.

From near the door, he winked at her. "See you in the morning. Sleep tight."

"Goodnight," she called softly.

A moment later, he was gone.

And it was only as Nick disappeared that Laura realised with an awful suddenness that something was terribly wrong. At first she couldn't quite work out what the problem was, it was just a vague sense that things weren't really as good as they had seemed when he was kissing her.

She didn't really have the right to feel this happy.

The nurse proceeded to take her temperature, and just as she slipped the clip on her finger to check her pulse Laura remembered.

For heaven's sake! Nick had been acting like a lover and for a short while she'd been fooled. She'd been drowsy and not thinking straight.

The nurse held up two fingers. "How many do you see?"

"Two," Laura told her, and received a nod of approval.

Oh, good grief. She could see and think perfectly clearly now, and for crying out loud, how had she forgotten that Nick was terminally allergic to love?

She'd had a bang on the head and the first thing she'd done when she came to was to let him kiss her senseless.

Fool!

He was brilliant at kissing her, expertly, beautifully... But that certainly didn't mean anything significant. Nothing to get excited about.

Last night he'd rejected her Big Offer.

He'd spent the day finding ways to back clear out of her life.

The nurse frowned as she filled in Laura's chart. "That young man is not doing you any good at all," she muttered.

And, miserably, Laura had to agree with her.

She was given two small white pills in a paper cup.

"These will help you to sleep."

Obediently she took the tablets. Somehow she knew that without them there would be no chance of a peaceful night's sleep.

"I want to go home," she told the doctor next morning, but he only smiled and murmured something about being a good girl and another twenty-four hours of observation.

A good girl? As the white coat marched out of her room Laura punched her pillow. ''I've been a good girl all my life.'' She was tired of obeying the rules.

Her life was one long row of ticks for being a boring good girl.

If only she could break the old mould.

Tears threatened. It was time for some drastic action. She would have to start with the hardest step—exterminating any wayward, undisciplined thoughts about Nick Farrell.

She was so busy staring at the ceiling and plotting a daring, new, Farrell-free life for herself that at first she didn't notice the person who suddenly lumbered into her room.

When she did see him, she blinked. Twice.

Her visitor had a bright red nose, incredibly curly orange hair and awkward overlong shoes.

Laura raised a hand to shade her eyes. She felt a surge of dismay. Surely the doctors had made a wrong diagnosis. There was something wrong with her head after all. She was seeing

272   THE WEDDING DARE

things. She had to be. Nobody wandered around in a hospital dressed like a...

A clown.

Adrenaline jolted through her, making her heart leap as she peered at her visitor more closely.

In addition to the nose and the hair, the clown's face was covered in traditional circus make-up and he was wearing a red and white striped shirt with a purple and black spotted bow-tie. His overalls were bright blue with colourful patches on the knees and he wore long, black clown shoes.

''I thought you might need cheering up,'' the clown said in a voice she immediately recognised.

A querulous hammering started in her chest. ''Nick, what on earth are you doing here dressed like that?''

Without answering, he grinned cheekily, plucked some apples and oranges from her fruit bowl and began to juggle them. Almost immediately an apple fell to the floor and rolled under her bed.

Shrugging, he returned the rest of the fruit to her bowl and scratched his orange hair. "I've been told by someone whose opinion I hold in high regard that hospital patients appreciate this sort of entertainment. Perhaps you'd prefer some acrobatics?"

Before she could answer, Nick tried for a handstand, but there clearly wasn't enough space. For a dangerous moment it looked as if his legs would end up out of the window or his whole muscle-packed body would crash-land on top of Laura's bed. He was forced to drop back to his feet very quickly.

"Sit down before you do yourself or this room some damage," Laura implored him, laughing.

With a dramatic sigh, he lowered himself into the chair beside her bed and leaned forward. "Let's do this the boring way. How are you this morning, Laura?"

"I'm perfectly fine," she said, but it was a lie. She felt as fragile as fine crystal. What on earth was Nick trying to do to her? "But for heaven's sake..." She gestured helplessly at his clothes.

He pulled a book from a pocket in his voluminous overalls. "I've also been told by someone who's an expert in this area that patients like to have stories read to them."

Laura could see his grey eyes twinkling through the clown paint. His gorgeous, dreamy eyes.

Hold your horses, girl! Don't forget that falling for Nick is a fast track to misery.

She turned her head away and spoke to the opposite wall. "Don't do this to me, Nick."

"Don't do what?"

"Don't play games." *Don't be charming and fun.* "Don't make me—" She'd been about to say, *Don't make me love you,* but just in time she bit the words back.

Nick dragged his chair a little closer and spoke softly. "So do you want to hear my story?"

In spite of her fears, Laura felt unbearably curious. Without risking a look at him, she asked, "Is it a story you've made up?"

"Sure."

"About a princess?"

"A prince. I thought it was time he got a story of his own."

A *prince?* Laura closed her eyes. *Why did she think this was going to be about Nick?*

The skin on her arms erupted into goose-bumps as she tried to answer lightly. "I guess a prince is a new angle. Does he live in a castle or a grass hut in the jungle?"

"This one is locked away in a high tower."

"The victim of a wicked witch?"

"The victim of his own—*fears.*"

"I see," she said quietly while her nervous system switched to maximum alert. "So the prince lives in the tower by himself? No visitors? No princesses?"

After a moment, Nick answered, "The only people he lets in are jesters."

"They can be fun."

"Sure. And from time to time he does something silly and reckless and his friends cheer and clap."

Laura's tense fingers gripped at the bed sheet. Nick was definitely talking about himself. "What's the main plot development? Where's the complication?"

She braved a quick glance Nick's way and his eyes were suspiciously bright as he said, "A little redheaded bird with amazing blue feathers flew up to his window. He thought she was just a harmless bird, so…" He shrugged and slanted her a crooked little smile. "So he chatted to her."

Laura couldn't bear this. What game was Nick playing? Couldn't he guess what this was doing to her?

She sank back into the pillow and closed her eyes again, but hot tears slipped beneath her eyelashes and ran down her cheeks. She dabbed at her face with the sheet. "A harmless bird?" she croaked. "Where's the threat in that?"

"Laura," he murmured, and suddenly his voice sounded as choked and raspy as hers. She felt his knees nudge the bed as he leaned even closer. "If she was really a harmless little bird there'd be no problem at all."

Laura couldn't reply.

After some time, she heard Nick clear his throat. "Problem was…" he began, and then there was another pause. Three long sec-

onds...four...five agonising seconds of silence.

"Problem was," he said at last, "she was
in disguise. She was really a gutsy, big-
hearted, dragon-slaying, perfect-in-every-way
princess."

Now she definitely couldn't take any more
of this game-playing. Laura turned towards
Nick and sobbed, "Cut the story. Just give it
to me straight, Nick. What are you trying to
tell me?"

He reached for her hand. "I'm here to say
thank you. The risk you took yesterday..."

Just in time Laura stifled her cry of disappointment. *He was here to say thank you.*

That was what all this was about! Heck, if
he only wanted to say thank you, she would
have preferred a quick phone call. Maybe a
box of chocolates.

But Nick had gone to all this trouble just to
offer his thanks.

What kind of soft-headed fool was she to
have been thinking about something more?
She'd been nursing a ludicrous hope that at
some time in the past twenty-four hours this

man had changed. No matter how hard she tried to be sensible she kept thinking about how she actually wanted to spend the rest of her life with him.

''There's no need to go to so much trouble to thank me,'' she replied dully. ''I can't take too much credit. That kind of do-good stuff comes instinctively to me. It's in my genes.''

''Then I'm in debt to your ancestors.''

Her lips pursed into a tight little circle. Then she shrugged and suddenly felt terribly, unbearably tired.

Nick cleared his throat. ''Actually, there is something else I want to tell you.''

''You'll need the keys to my house to pick up the rest of the girls' things?''

''No. Well, I guess I might do that at some stage, but what I wanted to say was a touch more personal.''

''Oh?'' When she saw the shimmer of deep emotion in Nick's eyes, the tiredness left her in a flash. ''I'm listening.''

He suddenly dropped his gaze to the floor and shook his head. ''I—I stand in court all day and spout all kinds of nonsense, and quite often it has serious implications for other people's lives. And now I want to say the most important sentence of *my* life and I'm stage-struck. Shaking in my boots.''

Just one sentence?

Laura felt as if her heart was tripping down a long flight of stairs. She could feel each painful bounce. It hurt so badly.

''One little sentence?'' she whispered, and a corner of her mouth lifted into the bravest of tiny half-smiles. ''I *dare* you to say it.''

''Dare?'' He looked at her quickly, then suddenly his eyes flashed and he grinned as he pulled off his clown nose. His own nose looked tanned and decidedly noble amidst all the white clown paint.

''OK, here goes.'' He took a deep breath. ''Laura Goodman, I love you—I never knew it was possible to love another human being as much as I love you.''

''Oh, Nick,'' Laura cried.

His eyes shone damply.

She couldn't help asking, ''Do you really mean it?''

"Ouch." He flinched. "I guess I deserve that." With long brown fingers, he prised her hand from its death grip on the bed sheet and massaged her fingers gently. "I'm very sure I love you, Laura. You know how hard I've fought against falling for you. But I couldn't help it; it happened anyhow."

He pressed his lips to her hand. "You're just so inescapably lovable."

Laura could hardly see Nick through her own tears.

"Is that OK?" he asked. "If I tell you I love you, is that a problem?"

"No problem," she whispered. "No problem at all." She sat up a little straighter. "But what made you change your mind?"

His mouth quirked into a lopsided grin. "It finally sank in to my slow brain that I was game enough or stupid enough to strip off my clothes, but I wasn't prepared to strip away my emotions—to discover how I really felt about—you."

Deep inside, Laura was singing. She could feel happiness pushing its way to the surface. Only one thing was holding it down. She needed to be sure Nick wasn't confusing love with guilt. "Was last night—like Miranda's accident all over again?"

Nick's face grew tight and he looked away for moment. "Yes and no."

In heart-hammering silence, she waited for him to explain.

"You must understand that I'm not the same bloke who developed a crush on the prettiest girl in Atherton High at the age of sixteen."

He moved to sit beside her on the bed and tucked a stray curl behind her ear. "I did love Miranda with all the zeal of immaturity, and I was sad when I lost her, but so much of that was tied up with guilt."

"It's not like that now?"

"Laura, after I dragged myself from your house the other night I was utterly miserable, but I kept telling myself that my feelings were simply lust. But yesterday, when you phoned to tell me Stokes was tailing you, I suddenly realised the truth. I've been falling in love with you ever since the night we met when you were wearing those ridiculous feathers."

He touched her cheek with shaking fingers. "Last night, when I thought I'd lost you, I wanted to lie down and die right next to you. I was completely destroyed. You have no idea how much I need you in my life."

She had things she wanted to say but her throat was blocked by tears.

"So what do you think?" Nick asked shyly.

Laura snuffled and coughed and fiddled with his clown's bow-tie. "I think you know that I've been pretty much in love with you since the first time I saw you in a clown suit."

He looked relieved and amused. "It took you that long? So you want me to stay in this kind of get-up for ever?"

With a slow grin, she asked, "You really want to know what I'd like?"

"Of course."

Grabbing a handful of tissues from the pack on the bedside table, she wiped the make-up from his mouth.

Nick was a bright boy. He could take a hint. And, without a word, his make-up-free lips settled over hers and once again Laura was experiencing Nick Farrell style magic. Bliss.

When they came up for air, she whispered, "I really like you as a clown, but I think I fancied you even more as a stripper."

His eyes widened with amused surprise.

"You wouldn't strip for me now, would you?"

"What?" Nick looked incredulous and sent an anxious glance over his shoulder. "Here in this hospital?"

"You're not the only one who's changed, Nick. I'm often in a daring mood these days. We can close the door. Anyhow, medical people see naked bodies every day. I rather like the idea of all those bits of clown costume coming off one by one..."

"The whole way?"

She smiled and raised a questioning eyebrow and he shook his head and chuckled. "You're daring me again, aren't you? How about a guaranteed private performance at home?"

The very thought made Laura sizzle, but she pretended to think it over. "I guess I could settle for that."

"OK. You're on, but there's one condition."

"What's that?"

"Marry me."

"Oh…"

Laura stared at Nick. His handsome features were covered in messy, smudged paint, but his eyes… His eyes were full of love and longing and they told her everything she wanted to know.

"You see, that's another thing I've found out about myself," he said with a warm smile. "I need to let the whole world know you're mine. I really want to get married, Laura."

"Yes," she whispered.

"Yes?" he repeated. "Is that yes, you'll marry me?"

"What did you expect, Nick? Look at me. I'm positively drooling at the thought of being your wife."

She was rewarded with another of Nick's seriously expert kisses. As he nuzzled her sexily, he asked, "You haven't forgotten that my daughters are a kind of permanent attachment?"

"Of course I haven't. I love your little girls almost as much as I love their daddy." And, just to prove it, she reached up to kiss him again. A deep, hungry kiss, full of seductive promise.

"Can you hang on just a tick?" Nick eventually muttered. Without waiting for her answer, he stood up and crossed the room. Ducking his head around the door, he gave a thumbs-up sign to someone down the hall.

The next minute there was a scurry of running feet and two little bodies hurtled into the room.

"Did she say yes?" Kate and Felicity shouted simultaneously.

Nick beamed at them. "She did."

"What's been going on?" Laura cried. "A conspiracy?"

Kate rushed to hug Laura while Felicity danced around the room with excited skips accompanied by war hoops of delight.

"You're going to marry Daddy!"

"You're going to be our mummy!"

"I'm so relieved," Kate whispered to Laura. "I told Daddy you would never want to marry him if he asked you while he was dressed up like a clown.''

Laura laughed. ''Your father happens to know I'm rather fond of clowns.''

''Do you think you will need a flower girl at your wedding?''

Laura hugged Kate with one arm and reached out towards Felicity with the other. ''I think I'll definitely need two flower girls.''

''In pink dresses,'' crowed Felicity.

''No, blue,'' corrected Kate.

''One of each?'' suggested Nick. He winked at Laura and her heart did a weird little duck dive from feeling so much happiness all at once.

Felicity looked at Laura intently. ''Has Daddy kissed you yet?'' She studied Laura's glowing face. ''Oh, goody, he has. You've got clown paint on your nose.'' Letting out a happy, relieved sigh, the little girl sent a beaming smile around the room to her father, her sister and Laura. ''Everything is going to be perfect now.''

''Yes,'' agreed Laura. ''Everything will be perfect.''

She smiled up at Nick. She loved these little girls and she was going to marry their father— the sexiest clown-cum-stripper in the world.

What could be more perfect than that?

MILLS & BOON® PUBLISH EIGHT LARGE PRINT TITLES A MONTH. THESE ARE THE EIGHT TITLES FOR JUNE 2002

❧

A SECRET VENGEANCE
Miranda Lee

THE ITALIAN'S BRIDE
Diana Hamilton

D'ALESSANDRO'S CHILD
Catherine Spencer

DESERT AFFAIR
Kate Walker

THE ENGAGEMENT EFFECT
Neels & Fielding

THE ENGLISHMAN'S BRIDE
Sophie Weston

THE BRIDEGROOM'S VOW
Rebecca Winters

THE WEDDING DARE
Barbara Hannay

MILLS & BOON®

Makes any time special™